"This story is well told, with a fast pace, lots of action, and plenty of unanswered questions at the end to justify the sequel."

—KIRKUS REVIEWS

SOMETHING'S LURKING IN THE DARK. . . .

A hard snout nudged up against Adam's ear and breathed out. The warning rasp of its breath was like sandpaper on his senses. Adam stopped talking, clamped his teeth down on his lower lip and tried to stop shaking. He was half grateful to the darkness for hiding most of this thing, yet terrified by the thought of what else might be lurking—

Something moved to his right.

The shadowy shape growled menacingly. It sniffed the air as it padded about the cave—and suddenly, a fierce yellow glare spat from spotlights in the rocky ceiling. *Lights? Where did the lights come from?* Adam screwed up his eyes, blinked as his vision slowly adjusted.

Then, as the monster stood fully revealed at last, he wished they hadn't.

A dinosaur was glaring down at him.

A living, breathing, dark-green dinosaur. Like a T. rex.

THE HUNTING: BOOK 1

Z. REX

STEVE COLE

SCHOLASTIC INC.

New York Toronto London Auckland
Sydney Mexico City New Delhi Hong Kong

FOR TOBEY

ISBN 978-0-545-31417-6

12 11 10 9 8 7 6 5 4 3 2 1   10 11 12 13 14 15/0

Printed in the U.S.A.   40

First Scholastic printing, October 2010

ACKNOWLEDGMENTS

This one's been quite a ride, and scaly, dinosaur-sized thanks are due to . . . Michael Green—for saying yes and pushing me in the right direction. Courtenay Palmer and Kiffin Steurer—who've watched out for Zed and me. Philippa Milnes-Smith—for all the deals and all she deals with. Jill Cole, my wife—for everything she does.

OHUN**TER**

The creature had no name. There was nothing like it on Earth.

But tonight it would show everyone what it could really do.

Massive and powerful, the creature smashed a path through the moonlit forest. It tore apart the brushwood, uprooting tall trees that had stayed standing for hundreds of years. Its night vision brought a bloodred tint to the shadow landscape.

It was hunting.

Supernatural senses had already pierced the skin of its prey like great, invisible fangs. The creature scented hot blood coursing through veins. Heard the stroke of limbs brushing together. Felt the currents in the air swirling around its victim. With every splintering stride, the picture became clearer. . . .

The hunting creature did not know why its target had been chosen for death this night. But killing was something it did exceptionally well.

There. In the forest clearing, in the darkness, its prey was hiding. Keeping stock-still.

As if that might save it.

A triumphant roar built in the hunter's throat. The undergrowth exploded around it as it flew like a living missile toward its victim, baring gleaming, knife-point teeth. . . .

Less than a second later, the creature held its prey in its snapped-shut jaws.

Mission accomplished.

The perfect kill.

A small group of people were waiting, watching, wondering as the creature returned. "An impressive result," said one onlooker softly. "We're ready to move to the next phase."

The creature sensed the fear and excitement mingling in its audience. It turned away, looking back into the forest. A forest that it might once have called home, far away and long ago.

Then the creature stalked over to the man who had spoken, looming over him. With a flick of its thick tongue, it spat the remains of its victim at his feet.

1 REALITY

Adam Adlar kicked down the door and burst into the darkness beyond it. He paused for a moment, marveling that he felt no pain in his foot, only a pleasing thrill of strength. Then a low growl sounded from the thick shadows ahead of him. Something large had been cooped up in here, something deadly. But Adam knew he could take it. He knew—

"DIE, INTRUDER!" A monstrous, twisted figure lunged at him from out of the shadows, its red eyes glinting, its terrifying claws scrabbling for his face. Adam hurled himself under the creature's arms. With his head tucked down, he hit the stone floor on his shoulder, his momentum carrying him into a perfect forward roll that left him back on his feet a moment later. Exulting in his power and agility, he twirled back around and landed a brutal karate chop to the monster's side, cracking its ribs like brittle chalk.

Ignoring the creature's agonizing scream, barely pausing for breath, Adam launched into his favorite fight moves, which were now as natural to him as breathing, a stomp kick followed by a jab cross. He lashed out with his left foot, sending the creature staggering backward, and followed up with right and left jabs in rapid succession, fists smacking into hard flesh. The monster wasn't getting back up from that combo.

Every sense wired and buzzing, Adam charged onward into the gloom and found another door. He booted it, feeling the jolt in his foot, but this time the door didn't open. He kicked again, and then again even harder, but the door wouldn't give an inch.

"Come on!" he yelled, frustration edging into fear as wet, scraping, slobbering noises started up behind him and the stench of rotten meat filled his nostrils. "Dad, this isn't fair!" He spun back around, hoping to find another exit from the enemy's lair before it was too late. A low, gurgling chuckle carried from the dark. Taloned fingers closed around his throat, squeezed tighter, tighter. Adam felt a wave of nausea, a rush of oncoming darkness—

GAME OVER.

And Adam was back on the couch in the testing lab, soaked with sweat and panting for breath, half terrified, half ecstatic. Exiting Ultra-Reality was more like waking from a vivid, incredible dream than quitting a game. For a moment he wasn't sure which was reality, this windowless industrial unit in New Mexico or the dark, digital lair he'd left behind. But as his racing heart slowed, Adam took in the Ultra-Reality console— its staring green bulb extinguished now—and his dad standing over him, carefully pulling the heavy headset from his temples and the sensor pads from his fists and feet.

"Wow," said Adam groggily. "That was awesome, the realest ever. You're a genius, Dad—"

"C'mon now, take it easy," Mr. Adlar soothed him in his warm Midwestern accent. "Get your breath back."

"You are, though." Adam wasn't just being loyal; when the bugs were fixed, he knew that U-R would be the ultimate gaming experience. The console turned thoughts into computer commands and game code into things you could feel. Instead of using a controller or waving your arms, you could just *think* what you wanted a character to do, really become the hero. In an instant, Adam could transform from a skinny, dark-haired Edinburgh teen into a blond, muscular monster slayer surrounded by admiring girls and sidekicks. And thanks to the sensor pads, you could even feel an impression of the impact of blows and footfalls. Ultra-Reality lived up to its name.

"I was following your gameplay on screen." His dad

looked concerned. "What happened with that door you couldn't open?"

"I don't know," said Adam. "Was it me? Did your favorite test subject mess up?"

"My *only* test subject," Dad reminded him evenly. "The Think-Send technology—"

"Copyright and trademark, Bill Adlar."

"—was modeled on your brain waves. Right now, the game wouldn't work at all with anyone else playing it."

Adam watched his father's forehead furrow into deep, familiar creases. He remembered that when Mum was still around, his dad seemed always to be smiling. Each new triumph had sent him dancing around the room, playing air guitar till his glasses fell off. Although born in Michigan, he'd gone to Edinburgh to do his postdoctorate in computer science and fallen in love with the place—and with Adam's mum. They'd started a family there, he'd had a nice income from dozens of patents, and life must have seemed pretty good.

That was then, and this is now, Adam thought. Mum had died four years ago, and Dad had thrown himself ever further into his work perfecting Ultra-Reality. But developing a new games system wasn't cheap, especially one as groundbreaking as U-R. And since the really big players had passed on it—"too ambitious," they'd said—Mr. Adlar had been forced to work with smaller companies. So far, these firms had always run out of funding before he could deliver the goods, and Adam had watched his dad grow grayer and gaunter with each setback.

"I dunno. . . ." Adam shrugged. "Maybe I didn't imagine what I wanted to do hard enough?"

Mr. Adlar shook his head. "I'll go through the command translator log, see if any glitches jump out at me."

"Do you think you'll be finished before we have to get back to Edinburgh?" Adam smiled. "I mean, if it's any help, I don't mind missing the start of school—"

"We've only got the lease on the apartment till the third week of August," Mr. Adlar murmured. "Frankly, I doubt I'll still be here by then. There was a lot riding on today's test. If it's back to the drawing board . . ." He forced a smile. "Aw, what the hell, it's not the end of the world. I have other irons in the fire."

Adam raised his eyebrows. "You mean another company's interested in taking on Ultra-Reality?"

His dad hesitated. "Well, in developing some of the key technology, anyway. It's a research center called Fort Ponil—someone I used to work with got in touch. They're fairly local, based outside Los Alamos. We're meeting this evening with a couple of suits to discuss it."

"Oh, right." Adam couldn't hide his disappointment. "So, I've got microwave pizza for one *again* to-night, huh?"

"Sorry." Mr. Adlar ruffled Adam's hair. "But you know, it won't be forever."

o   o   o

Adam was soon outside on his bike in the afternoon glare, pedaling away from the ugly steel warehouse unit. The asphalt roads shimmered in the heat like dark canals as he made his way back to the apartment in a soulless, purpose-built modern block just outside the gates to the industrial park. Black Mesa, the vast, flat-topped mountain that straddled three states, loomed darkly over the arid plains beyond the chain-link fences.

The whole high-tech development felt out of place here in the epic wilderness beyond Santa Fe. Most of the buildings in these parts looked old even if they weren't. He'd even seen gas stations disguised as ancient Native American monuments, trying to blend in. It felt wrong somehow to see industry here on show in all its sharp-angled sleekness. Adam felt a twinge of longing for the rainy skies and blackened sandstone of Scotland—followed immediately by the fear that he might be flying back there alone. He was thirteen now, not a kid, and Dad had made mutterings in the past about sending him to boarding school or to distant relatives in England. Neither option appealed much to Adam, but what could he do? He never had much say in what Dad did.

He gritted his teeth and pedaled faster. Sometimes he wished he could disappear into a virtual world where he won all the fights and just stay there.

o   o   o

Adam spent the night eating pizza and riffling through a bunch of new games for his Xbox. Five weeks here and he still wasn't comfortable. The second-floor apartment was more like a show home than somewhere you'd actually live. Lacking in furniture as well as charm, it felt hollow, impersonal. No one else lived in the building, so when Dad was away the loneliness was overwhelming.

Mr. Adlar finally made it back after midnight. Adam could tell at once that something interesting had gone down. His dad seemed distracted, a bundle of nervous energy, but he was trying not to show it. That had to mean he was hopeful—Adam knew his dad's moods better than he knew his own.

"So, how'd it go?" asked Adam, switching off the TV.

"Not much to tell at this stage," Mr. Adlar said cagily, perching on the edge of the sofa. "But there could be. They're doing amazing things, things you wouldn't believe. . . ." He drummed his fingers on the arm of the sofa. "The organization's bigger than I thought. They've got facilities all over the world—including one not a million miles from Edinburgh."

"Yeah?" Adam perked up. "Sounds perfect!"

"Not exactly. First, I need to find out more about . . . the project." He looked at Adam. "You can look after yourself, right, Ad? If I have to leave you on your own for a bit?"

Here we go, thought Adam. "Why?"

"I've arranged a short leave of absence with my current partners—'cause if I want to secure a place with these guys, I've got to stay at Fort Ponil for a couple of nights. Work on some top secret stuff. Show how indispensable I can be."

If it means we can both stay in Edinburgh, I'll put up with anything, thought Adam. "Look, I'm used to your work keeping you tied up for days. I can handle it. I'm big enough."

"And ugly enough," his dad agreed.

Adam grinned. "Plus, it means I can stay up as late as I like. Bring it on!"

"Bring it on. . . . Right." Mr. Adlar stared into space. "Thanks, Adam. It'll only be for two or three days, tops."

o o o

Mr. Adlar left the next morning in the big, black Cadillac sent to collect him. Adam put on a brave face and waved his father off. But he didn't like the look of the car. As it pulled away down the quiet, dust-blown street, it reminded him of a hearse.

The sedan disappeared with his dad into the distant mountains, which were glowing bloodred in the morning sun.

2 DESTRUCTION

Dad!" Adam woke up from the nightmare, shouting for his father. Then he remembered how things were and let his head fall back against the pillow. No sense in wasting his breath.

"Day nine on my own," he muttered.

Rubbing sleep from his eyes, he padded through the darkened apartment to Dad's room, unable to resist checking. *Maybe he came back in the night,* Adam thought. *Maybe this time—*

The door stood wide open. The bed was empty and unmade. A brown leather briefcase lay where he'd kicked it the night before.

Nothing had changed. Dad still wasn't back.

Adam went back to his bedroom to work out his next

move. It would probably involve playing his Xbox. He hadn't done much else since Dad had disappeared. He checked the clock. It was five A.M. He must have dozed off around one-thirty, still in his jeans and T-shirt. The High Scores league table filled the wide screen, his name alone listed again and again.

Adam knew his mates back home in Scotland would be jealous of the life he'd been living—his own place, own space, a cookie jar full of cash, an endless supply of delivery food, no nags or hassles or *Time for bed*s. . . . But right now, he was sick of freedom.

You've got some serious sucking up to me to do when you get back, Dad.

Yawning, Adam crossed to the window. The stars were fading as the first peeps of sun warmed up New Mexico, slowly lifting the mountains' shadows. Then he caught a sudden movement some way off, like a ripple on the air—as if something had just flitted across the sky at impossible speed. He stared hard into the brightening orange of daybreak, but didn't see the movement again.

"Great," Adam murmured. "Now I'm losing it."

He'd started talking to himself a lot since Dad had gone. He'd spent the days gaming, cycling around the lonely industrial park and bugging his friends back in Edinburgh on Instant Messenger. At least *they* hadn't totally forgotten him. And he'd gone to bed each night listening out for his father, hoping to catch the turn of the key and the front door squeaking open. But the night remained stubbornly silent, loaded with uneasy dreams.

Yesterday, for want of something better to do, he'd tried hanging out around Dad's workplace here in the industrial park. But the team who'd used to joke around with him as their resident "test case" weren't so friendly now. It turned out that their unit had been broken into a couple of days ago, with tons of gear nicked. And just the next day, Adam's dad had told them he wouldn't be coming back to work in the near future.

"Inventors don't care about anyone," railed one of Dad's old team. "They live in a world of their own."

At least he bothered to tell you, Adam had thought, *instead of leaving you to work it out for yourselves. He could be dead for all I know.*

Adam flung himself back onto his bed and switched the TV over to News 24 for some company. The Scottish anchorman was on in the mornings, which made Adam feel a little less homesick. Clearly not much had been happening in the world, as all the talk was of a film star couple breaking up and some rubbish about a giant monster spotted in a state park in southern Utah. Nothing exactly serious.

But what if something serious had happened to his dad?

Mr. Adlar had started off calling and mailing as he usually did when he was working away. Then, three days in, a single text message marked the end of all that: *Can't get away. Friends of mine will look in on you soon. Love, Dad.*

Adam had been disappointed but not too worried; this wasn't the first time Dad had become too caught up in his work to talk, feeling himself close to a big breakthrough. It was a pain, but if it led to a contract with these Ponil people back in Edinburgh . . .

He'd nursed the hopeful thought through days four and five, though Dad's occasional texts had given little encouragement.

And then Dad's promised friend had turned up— some guy with the stiff, solid bearing of a soldier or security man and the name Frankie Bateman. He was a large, powerfully built guy, formidable looking despite the beer gut hanging over his waistband. "I'm from Fort Ponil. Your dad asked me to look in on you." Bateman's thick mustache bristled above the confident smile, and his all-American voice was as deep as the dimple on his chin. "You know, see how you're doing."

"When's Dad coming home?" Adam had asked.

"Real soon." Bateman kept smiling.

"Can't I come and visit?"

"We're actually getting you security clearance right now. Shouldn't take much longer."

"Security clearance?" Adam frowned. "Sounds like the military."

"Nothing like that, really." Bateman pushed his way inside. "Meantime, your dad asked me to pick up some stuff for him. . . ."

The big man spent ages in Mr. Adlar's room, but came out with nothing but a few clothes and a sour look. Then he brought in a stack of groceries from the car, and even unpacked it while Adam watched TV. "Don't eat it all at once, y'hear?" Bateman held up Adam's Nokia. "Oh, and nice cell phone by the way. . . . I've got my eye on one like this."

"Yeah, it's all right," said Adam, though in truth it was nothing special. Bateman had put down the phone and left, promising to check in again in a couple of days.

That had been three days ago. "Chances are, big Frankie's coming today," Adam announced out loud. "And if he does, I'll *make* him take me to Fort Ponil, security clearance or not. He can drop me in the street if he wants, but I'm going. . . ."

His words sounded stupidly small in the big apartment.

Suddenly, a tremor rattled the pile of dirty dishes in the sink. *Weird,* Adam thought. Even the biggest trucks turning into the industrial park didn't normally shake the place like that.

He crossed to the cupboard to get out a bowl for cereal, and noticed his mobile phone on the counter.

One new message, it said, and the words jolted

through Adam like fifty thousand volts. He grabbed the phone, saw his dad's number, saw the text had been sent almost an hour ago. A mixture of relief and anger washed through him. "Nothing at all for ages, then you can't even be bothered to call and—"

Just as he was about to access the message, the TV switched off. Adam frowned. His digital clock had blinked off too. Maybe the tremor had taken out the local power supply. "Freakin' fabulous," Adam muttered. "That's *really* going to make things dull around here. . . ."

Then, as if laughing in his face, the tremor came again, much harder this time. It nearly knocked Adam off his feet. Was it an earthquake? Still holding the phone, he crossed quickly to the big picture window to check the street outside for damage. The apartment was two stories up, so if the building was about to collapse . . .

But as he approached the tinted glass, Adam heard a harsh squeal of brakes. A large, dark car had lurched to a stop outside the entrance to the complex, the same Cadillac that had taken his dad what seemed like a lifetime ago. Five men in suits scrambled out of the car like their butts were on fire.

One of them was Frankie Bateman. He wasn't smiling now.

Bit early, isn't it? thought Adam, his heart quickening as he watched Bateman gesture to the other men as though snapping out orders. *And why bring so many friends?* Uneasy now, he looked back at his phone, called up Dad's message—

Suddenly the whole building lurched and he was thrown so hard against the window he cracked the pane. He dropped the phone. In a daze, he saw the men outside were pulling guns from their jackets and staring around wildly. They started firing into the air.

Adam caught a glimpse of something dark and hazy, a fleeting shadow on reality. Then, impossibly, with a crushing boom of metal, the big black car collapsed in on itself, as if something huge and invisible had slammed on the roof with colossal force. The men in suits fired into the air, looking terrified. Another snatch of shadow movement and the crushed car went flying, rolling over and over in a suicide spin. It smashed into the entrance to the industrial park, buckling the metal gates, the crash of the impact drowning out the gunfire.

Adam stared down at the sudden carnage, fixed to the spot with fright, trying to make sense of what was happening. *What do those men think they're they shooting at?*

That same moment, the window shattered over him and the wall spat plaster at his face. Shards of glass fell from Adam's body and crunched under his sneakers as he snatched up the phone and bolted, terrified, to the other side of the apartment. *Whether they mean to or not,* he thought, *they're shooting at me!* He made to dial 911—but hitting the floorboards must've jogged the phone's battery. It had switched itself off. "Come on," he muttered, stabbing at the on button. With the window gone, everything was suddenly so much louder, like the world had turned up its volume control.

Even so, nothing prepared Adam for the roar.

It was like an express train thundering past. A wild, unearthly howl that sent vibrations hurtling through his bones. Total panic took hold. *Get out. You've got to get away.* But the madness down below was all happening outside the front doors; he'd never get out that way. . . .

Then Adam remembered the fire escape at the back of the building, an iron zigzag of steps and railings leading down to the ground. He stuffed the phone into his pocket, ran into his dad's bedroom. It felt like his heart was crawling up his throat. Where was the key to the balcony doors? He fell upon the bedside table, yanked open the drawer and emptied it on the bed— just as the balcony exploded inward with a boom that nearly burst his eardrums. He threw himself down behind the bed as brick-shrapnel, glass and wood splinters slashed through the room. Moaning with fear, he yanked the blanket over his head like a shield to deflect the worst of the debris. *This whole place is being demolished,* he realized. *And me with it, if I don't get out. NOW.*

The deadly rain subsided and Adam got back to his feet, shaking and staring. The whole rear wall had been wrenched away, the debris scattered across the street. The fire escape was a twisted relic left dangling like a broken paper chain. What earthquake had the power to do this?

Then, as the pale morning sun stared in at Adam like a startled eye, a chill jumped through him. That same smoky haze he'd spied before was rippling dead ahead, as if the air itself were flexing its muscles. Scraping, scrabbling sounds soon followed, the sound of something hard and heavy-duty gouging out the brickwork downstairs. The gunfire had stopped. Had the men run away or were they—

Suddenly, with a splintering crash, the bedroom floor started to give way beneath Adam's feet as more of the story below was bashed away. Dad's large pine dresser scraped across the sloping floorboards and went into free fall, thundering onto the asphalt twenty-two yards below. Adam ran for the door but too late. The floor tilted sharply and he lost his balance, tumbling headlong with the furniture toward the gaping hole in the wall and the sheer drop beyond.

3 SURVIVAL

Adam clawed at the wooden flooring, trying desperately to cling on. But a moment later, he found himself launched into empty space.

The realization screamed at him—*A fall from this height could kill me.*

In the same split second, Adam grabbed for the twisted remains of the fire escape. His fingers caught and closed around a rail. He gasped, body jerking in midair as he just barely stopped his fall.

The fire escape had been totaled, the last stretch of ladder completely torn away.

The same deafening roar as before bellowed out, this time from inside the building. Something was tearing through the ground floor, trashing everything. . . .

Adam's fingers were already numb from holding his weight dead in the air. Terrified, he reached for the next rung down, caught hold of it and tried to swing himself across so he'd be closer to the ground. But the rung slipped from his grip and he dropped down the last several meters to the pavement. The impact shook through his body but he staggered up, too scared to linger, and ran to where his mountain bike stood chained. As the sound of more gunfire zinged through the air at the front of the building, Adam tore at the chain's combination lock with trembling fingers until the catch jumped open. Then he chucked the chain away and swung himself onto the Iron Horse's saddle.

As he started to pedal away, he saw another black Cadillac speeding toward him along the long, dusty road that bisected the rugged plains this side of the complex. He waved frantically, relief flooding through him. Whoever it was, maybe they could get him away from here.

The Caddy skidded in a wide circle in front of him as the driver expertly pulled a hand brake turn. As it stopped, a tall, blond man leaped out from the backseat. "That's Adlar's kid!" he hollered. "Must've got past Bateman."

Another man, bald and burly, scrambled out from the passenger side. "They kind of have their hands full, wouldn't you say?" The bald man smiled coldly. "So you're Adam Adlar, right?"

"Right," Adam answered with a fresh stab of unease. "Did—did my dad send you?"

"Sure," sneered the first man, pulling out a handgun. "Him and the Easter Bunny."

Adam stared in horror. What in the world was going on?

And then a thick black shadow swooped overhead. In a heartbeat, Adam saw the men's hard faces twist in terror as they stared up at something above him. They hurled themselves to the ground—

A blink later, a cream-colored convertible dropped from the sky. It landed upside down with a deafening smack on the rear of the black car, crushing it. The windows of both vehicles exploded as the impact sent the Cadillac careening across the road, almost crushing the bald, burly man as he rolled aside to get away.

With a sick feeling, Adam recognized the convertible at once. It was his dad's rental car, an extravagant indulgence, left parked in the underground garage. So how could it have come flying over the top of the building like a tossed stone . . . ?

A grating, bone-shaking rumble started up. Adam spun back around to find the entire apartment complex starting to collapse. "No way," he breathed, too shaken to feel much other than a horrified fascination. Then he caught movement, realized that the first man was scrambling back up with his gun—

Jerking to life, Adam stood up on the pedals and powered away.

"Get back here, kid!" the man screamed.

Adam ignored him, clicking upward through ten gears in half as many seconds. Half deafened by the cacophony of falling concrete, he pushed himself faster, shooting out from behind the crumbling corner of the block. He glimpsed Bateman and a friend running for the hills, while the other suited man lay sprawled over the remains of the Caddy. Adam didn't stop. Broken bricks chased him across the road as his home, his whole world, came crashing down around him. But fear had numbed him and all he could think about was to keep on pedaling. Approaching the entrance to the industrial park, he swerved neatly and tightly through the gap in the battered gates, and only then did he risk a backward glance.

A split second later, Adam gripped the brakes, jamming the wheels, almost hurling himself over the handlebars.

What. Is. THAT—?

A cloud of thick white dust shrouded the space where the apartment building once stood. But the powder seemed to be settling impossibly in midair to reveal the hideous outline of a monster standing astride the debris, as big as a bus. Adam glimpsed what could have been a thick, snaking tail, a ridged back, a huge reptilian head. Then the dust was shaken away with a bestial roar that nearly burst his eardrums and all suggestion of a monster seemed to vanish.

In blind panic, Adam pedaled away with a strength he never knew he possessed, his tires singing over the tarmac. He remembered that so-called news story: Giant monster spotted in southern Utah. Suddenly it didn't seem so crazy anymore.

He hung a reckless left turn at the first junction he came to, and then turned right, desperate to put cover and distance between him and the thing he had seen. Adam's calf muscles knotted as he pushed the pedals faster. His breath scraped in his throat. But over the noise of his flight he could hear the heavy pounding of footsteps behind him.

It's following.

Adam took another corner, leaning hard into the turn, chanced another look behind him. Nothing. But if the thing was invisible it could—

A blare of horns made Adam face front—to find a huge truck had pulled out from a junction just ahead of him. Adam knew he was going too fast to swerve aside or to stop in time. Instead, he threw himself from his saddle and dived underneath the trailer, between the two pairs of wheels. The jarring clang of his bike as it struck the undercarriage was an explosion in his ears. He landed heavily, crying out as he skidded across the asphalt.

For a second he lay dead still in shock. His body ached, burning in places like it was on fire, but he forced himself to scramble from beneath the truck and to his feet. The driver had thrown open the door, a big, burly, bearded guy looking anxious as he started out of the cab.

"No, don't. Stay where you are, please!" Adam limped quickly around to the passenger side and threw open the door. "We've got to get out of here."

"We?" The truck driver stared at him. "What are you talking about—?"

"That!" Adam stabbed a finger at one of the huge wing mirrors, which showed a view of the intersection behind them. The ripple in the air was turning darker, like a deepening, scaly scratch on the surface of reality. Again, Adam thought he could make out the outline of some hideous giant creature, but the faint form kept blurring into shapes that his mind couldn't make sense of.

The color had drained from the trucker's face as he slid back into his seat. "What is that thing?"

"Whatever it is, it's tearing up the whole neighborhood." Adam slammed the passenger door and belted up. "Please, get us out of here!"

From the way the trucker started whimpering, Adam guessed he'd got the message. Gunning the engine, the big man gripped the steering wheel and took the truck out onto the road. It accelerated away, but painfully slowly. Adam kept his eyes on the reflection, biting his lip as the weird, monstrous shadow creature pounded toward them. It was getting closer with every second. Any moment now it would catch up and then—

Suddenly a deeper note sounded in the bloodcurdling shriek—and whatever it was stopped coming. The sound of tearing metal carried down the empty street, and as the truck finally growled around the corner, Adam saw a massive chunk of corrugated iron sail through the air and land with a brutal crash.

The trucker crossed himself. "That looked like most of the factory roof."

Adam nodded slowly. "What kind of factory?"

"Meatpacking plant." The man's eyes were flicking constantly between the road ahead and the wing mirrors. "A thousand tons of poultry shipping through every day."

"Then if that thing could smell the raw meat . . ." Adam shook his head in a daze. "How about that—saved by dead chickens!" Somehow it didn't seem any less improbable than the rest of this morning's events.

"Where'd that roaring thing come from, anyway?" The trucker ran a sweaty hand through his hair. "Straight out of hell?"

Adam didn't say so, but he couldn't think of a more likely explanation.

4 MYSTERY

(W)ith a few miles stretching between the truck and the wreck of his rented home, Adam's adrenaline levels began to ebb. That was bad news on the injury front—suddenly he could feel every burn, bruise and scratch tattooing his body. He realized he looked a state: his jeans were ripped and dirty, his forehead was badly grazed and his arms were blackened with blood and oil from the tarmac.

But the pain couldn't keep deeper concerns from filling Adam's head. *All my stuff, buried and gone. . . . The rental car completely trashed. . . .* What *was* that monster? Was it coincidence that Bateman and his friends had come to get him at the same time it had decided to run amok?

And how did his dad figure in all this?

"You know, I never pick up hitchhikers, kid," the trucker growled, surlier now they were safely away. "Where am I dropping you?"

"I guess we need to tell the police what happened," said Adam.

"*We* nothing," the trucker said flatly. "I've got a haul to make on schedule. Can't afford to waste half the day jawing with a bunch of cops." He cleared his throat. "Anyway, got to be a normal explanation for all that—probably a movie crew. Special effects. Or one of those hidden camera shows where they film you and make you look like a jerk. . . . Well, I may've been pulling a week of all-nighters, but they won't get me that easy!"

Listening to the trucker do his best to dismiss all he had seen, Adam wished he could kid himself so easily. Then suddenly he remembered Dad's text on his phone. He pulled it from his pocket and keyed in the passcode. Then he swore as he noticed the battery was in the red; if the phone died before he could read the message . . .

Sucking at his cut fingers, Adam called it up:

Managed 2 steal back phone. Not me txting before. Them. Project wrong. Here now against will. Am being moved out. Get flight 2 Edinburgh. Give this web address to Jeff Hayden, Symtek Biotronics, BioQuarter— adlar65headspace.co.uk. Evidence there. Password ZREX.

Get evidence seen by right people who can take action. NO POLICE. Too risky. Promise I'll be OK. Josephs mad but needs me. Dad X.

Adam stared at the text, uncomprehending. Jeff Hayden was one of Dad's friends from way back at university, and the BioQuarter was the new science development in Edinburgh. But what did "Project wrong" mean—that it had gone wrong, or that it *was* wrong?

With his throat tightening, he wiped crossly at the tears in his eyes. *I've been strung along here for days by fake messages. Josephs must be Frankie Bateman's boss. He must have sent Bateman and his buddies to get me. But why?*

"Josephs mad," Adam muttered, scanning the message again. Did "mad" mean angry or insane? And what was that monster thing all about? *Oh, Dad. . . .* He swallowed hard. *What're you mixed up in? What's happened to you?*

"You even listening to me, kid?" the trucker rumbled. "C'mon, I said d'you want me to drop you at the nearest sheriff's office?"

Adam hesitated. NO POLICE, the text was yelling at him. He sighed and shook his head. "I need to get to the nearest airport."

"The *airport*?" The trucker scowled and slowed his rig, pulling in to the side of the road. "There's one at Los Alamos, but I'm no free taxi service." He pointed at a road leading off from the highway. "Gray Rock's a mile or so that way. Maybe you can pick up a bus from there."

"Okay." Adam pocketed his phone and stiffly opened the door. "Thanks for the ride."

"Happy hiking. And next time watch where you're going, hidden camera or no hidden camera!" the man yelled after him. "You could wind up the same way as your trashed bike!"

"That's what I'm afraid of," Adam muttered. "See ya." He slammed the door behind him and heard the truck growl away. The road ahead of him ran straight and seemingly forever, a gray scar through the scrubland. The mountains in the distance looked like dark creases in the otherwise faultless blue sky. Everything appeared so wide open, and he felt so tiny out here, mocked by the rugged calm of the new day.

In a single violent half hour he had lost everything. He'd been shot at, almost abducted, nearly killed. His bike had been mashed, his whole body hurt, and he was feeling scared to death. It was so tempting to give up, to drop in despair where he stood.

But if I do that, he thought, *I'll never get back up again. And I'll never find Dad.*

Step after painful step, Adam kept going.

o o o

It took less than an hour to reach the clean, quiet streets of Gray Rock. It was a small town laid out thinly over the wilderness. The buildings were low-rise, a messed-up mix of old-style Spanish and modern ugliness. Red clay walls clashed with neon signs. Spotless churches stood serenely beside boarded-up shops and battered motels. Not wanting to drain his phone any faster, Adam kept his eyes peeled for anywhere that might offer free internet connection. He had access to his dad's PayPal account from buying retro games off eBay; he had no idea if you could buy plane tickets that way, but he had to give it a try.

But . . . leave you behind, Dad? Wherever it is you are?

Fear for his father kept the sweat icy cold as he tramped through the rising heat.

A waitress in Lotaburger directed him to a library that she thought might have computers. Adam waited in the shade outside for its doors to open, wiping dirt and dried blood from his cuts and grazes with spit and fingers. When he heard the door-lock turn, he nearly knocked over the hard-faced Latina librarian in his haste to push inside.

"Hey, what happened to you?" she called after him.

"I, er, had a cycling accident," Adam said. "Do you have the internet?"

The librarian looked at him dubiously. "You're scuffed up pretty bad. Maybe you should see a doctor?"

"I'm okay," he snapped. Then he took a deep breath, forced himself to chill out a little. The woman was only trying to help, and upsetting her would get him nowhere. "It looks worse than it is," he added. "Honestly."

"Not local, are you?" Her dark eyes were curious. "Where're you from?"

"Scotland." Adam thickened his accent a little. "Aye, just arrived in town from Edinburgh with my dad. Couldn't sleep, still jet-lagged, thought I'd check my emails. Only we ride on the left back home—I forgot and I had to swerve fast to avoid a truck. . . ."

The librarian must have bought his story; her face warmed with sympathy as she pointed to a door behind her. "Look, the bathroom's through there. Why don't you clean yourself up a bit? I'll go start the computer for you."

"Brilliant, thanks," said Adam. He went and washed his sore hands, then dabbed gingerly at his wounds with wet paper towels for a minute or so before re-emerging.

"Now you're less likely to bleed over the keyboard," the librarian said wryly, nodding to a PC on a desk in a corner. "Help yourself."

Adam smiled his thanks. Within moments he was sitting down and had called up a list of local airports. If he could fly from Los Alamos to the bigger airport at Albuquerque. . . .

Then, suddenly, with a sick rush, he realized he had no passport. It was buried now under tons of rubble. I'll have to go back, he thought dismally. It could take days to find it. And the police will be there, and they'll start asking questions, and—

He reined in his racing thoughts, tried to stay calm and think things through. "If Dad's got evidence on whatever's going down," he murmured, "perhaps there's something there that will help me find him."

Checking that the librarian was busy sorting through books at her desk and not about to poke her nose in, Adam took out his phone, used some of the now precious power left and checked the web address in his dad's SMS, which he typed into the PC.

The computer's processors creaked and whirred for a few moments. Then the screen went completely black save for a white box in which sat a flashing cursor.

"Enter weirdo password now," Adam surmised, an uneasy fizz of nerves creeping through his stomach. "Z . . . R . . . E . . . and X, the unknown."

He typed in the last letter and hit return.

After a second's hesitation, the page turned blood-red except for some small black letters, bunched together in the center of the screen like a clot. A shiver snaked along Adam's aching backbone as he made sense of the message:

NICE TRY, ADLAR.

"What . . . ?" Adam tried to click back onto the password page, but the screen had frozen. Frightened, angry and impatient, he kept clicking on the back arrow.

Until suddenly the computer whirred. For a second

the screen showed a monstrous, reptilian head, with massive jagged teeth. It looked like a dragon, or . . .

A dinosaur?

The picture was so real that Adam recoiled, as if the hideous creature could somehow smash through the monitor and get him.

Then the application abruptly quit and the screen went dark, like an eye closing. Adam sat very still, heart racing, as the memory of the thing he'd glimpsed in the dust and rubble of the apartment block burned back into his mind. Whatever that thing is, Dad must know about it, he thought numbly. But why isn't the web address working? A realization struck him with a shiver. Maybe this Josephs guy found out he'd texted me and did something—trashed the evidence Dad wanted Jeff Hayden to see. . . .

Adam closed his eyes, trying not to panic. His whole world had turned crazy. *So, tell me, Dad,* he thought, fists clenched, his nails digging into his palms. *What am I supposed to do now?*

5 FUGITIVE

Feeling sick, sore and helpless, Adam tried to reboot the computer. But it wouldn't start up again, as though something on that web page had crippled the hard drive.

The librarian must have noticed the blank screen. Her voice was sharp: "Hey, what did you do?"

"I dunno." Adam turned shiftily to face her. "It, uh, just crashed on me."

"Seems to be your day for crashes." She eyed his scrapes and grimaced. "Those cuts really do look bad. You should get them cleaned up properly. Is your dad at home now?"

Adam resisted the urge to laugh in her face. "No, he . . . he had to start work already. Outside of Los

Alamos." He hesitated. "Have you heard of a place called Fort Ponil?"

"*Fort* Ponil? Don't think so." The librarian considered. "D'you mean Ponil Canyon over in Colfax County—where they found the fossil dinosaur tracks?"

"What?" Adam frowned, the image of the reptile head on the screen still bright in his memory. *Never mind how impossible it is. There could be a link.* He jumped up and crossed to the librarian. "Do you have any info on this canyon?"

"It's probably mentioned in one of our dinosaur books." She directed him toward nonfiction. "Check out the ones with 560 on the spine. And then get *yourself* checked out at the local walk-in clinic—deal?"

o   o   o

Thirty minutes later Adam left the library feeling worse than ever. The librarian had given him directions to the clinic, but they hadn't really sunk in. The giant dinosaur roaming his thoughts had already torn them to shreds.

Who'd have thought that old words on gum-gray pages could spark so many vivid images?

It turned out that the tracks in Ponil Canyon had been made by a T. rex, some sixty-five million years ago. Several near-complete fossils of the creature had been dug up in New Mexico. *Maybe Dad meant to type T.REX in the text, not ZREX,* mused Adam. But even if he had, what evidence had the password been supposed to keep secure?

Tyrannosaurus rex was one of the largest carnivores to ever walk the Earth, a massive, meat-eating destroyer that evolved during the late Cretaceous period. One of the last dinosaurs to exist before whatever wiped them all out, it weighed around six tons, had powerful two-clawed hands and huge hind legs as thick as redwoods. Its teeth were close to a foot long.

You wouldn't want to meet it in a dark alley.

Or even in an industrial park.

I'm cracking up. Adam felt cold despite the blazing sun. *What am I thinking? That dinosaurs still exist?*

Tyrannosaurus rex meant "tyrant lizard king." It had the strongest bite of any carnivore, with jaws uniquely designed to help it rip maximum bone and tissue with a single snap. And while some experts figured the T. rex was a scavenger that fed on the dead, most declared it a hunter—one equipped to tackle the largest prey around. . . .

Adam grimaced and tried harder to recall the route to the clinic.

The sight of a phone booth distracted him for a moment. Maybe he could find the number for Jeff Hayden at this Symtek place. He had no cash, but if the operator could reverse the charges. . . .

He went inside the booth and dialed double-zero for

the international operator. Then he saw the phone cable had been cut.

Swearing under his breath, he decided to gamble the last bar of battery on his old Nokia. He searched for Symtek Biotronics online, but the browser was taking forever to load anything—and when it came to coping with the company's Flash animated home page, it seemed to give up altogether. "Come on," he muttered, shaking the phone uselessly. It bleeped a low-power message at him morosely, as if making excuses.

Crossly, Adam clicked back to his SMS folder and resolved to try again at the walk-in clinic. There was bound to be a phone.

A signpost and an old lady helped him on his way there. But as he threaded his way through the sunlit streets, he noticed people clocking his face, eyes lingering just a little too long. It made him feel weird.

Finally Adam reached the clinic. It was newly built at the edge of town and looked like something out of Toyland—single-story, blocky and white with a gray pointed roof. He pushed through the door into the welcome shade of a waiting room. A woman sat behind a counter, the scowl on her face seemingly as ingrained as the smell of lavender and disinfectant. Adam wondered how a kid with no passport, money or health insurance would be received. Then he shrugged. After all that had happened today, how scary could she be?

Adam lined up behind an elderly couple and watched the TV mounted on the wall, showing the local news to waiting patients.

"A freak tornado caused a trail of damage throughout the Brakspear Industrial Zone outside of Santa Fe early this morning," said the anchorwoman, and Adam felt a jolt go through him. The camera lingered lovingly on the crushed remains of his apartment block and his dad's trashed rental car. Adam swallowed hard as he relived the morning's mayhem. For those few seconds he was staring at the carcass of an old life, trampled suddenly to dust.

The cameras cut to the meatpacking plant next, its corrugated roof hanging off like a picked scab.

And then a photograph of Adam sprang onto the screen.

"What the . . . ?" Adam saw it was the picture Dad had taken last Christmas, the one he'd said he always kept on his desk. The world seemed to tilt sideways as the anchorwoman resumed her voice-over with new gravity.

"Police are pursuing a thirteen-year-old runaway, Adam Adlar, in connection with a spate of lootings in the wake of the tornado. Adlar is slightly built, around five foot five, speaks with a Scottish accent and may be armed. Anyone sighting him should alert police on this number . . ."

"No. . . ." Adam's voice was a choke in his throat as

anger, disbelief and fear fought to hold sway in his head. Those people in the street outside, staring at him . . . just as the woman at the counter was staring now, her frown starting to deepen.

Adam turned and ran out of the health center, crashing through the doors and back out into lurid daylight. His mind was racing as fast as his heart, but he forced himself not to run and draw any more attention. He walked through the parking lot and then hunkered down between a couple of four-by-fours, trying to gather his thoughts.

Bateman and those men were after me before that monster thing came, but I got away—so now they're trying to put the whole of New Mexico on my back, including the police. But why do they still want me if they've already trashed the evidence Dad's meant to have? He chewed his lip. Maybe the cops were in on his dad's kidnapping too. Maybe they knew about the invisible creature, knew it was no tornado but were trying to cover it up, reeling in any witnesses who might speak out.

He shivered as he thought back to his dad's text. Suddenly he was seeing *"No police . . . too risky"* in a different light.

Voices carried from the other side of the lot. Doors clunked open and shut. Adam expected to hear sirens at any moment. He couldn't risk giving himself up. It was time to split.

The parking lot edged onto an alien landscape of red prairie, interrupted only by coarse scrub bushes and a line of trees in the middle distance. With a deep breath and a muttered prayer to anyone who might be listening, Adam set off at a run for the wildness beyond Gray Rock.

6 MONSTER

Dusk was starting to fall as calmly as the dawn had risen some twelve hours earlier. But it felt to Adam as if he'd lived a lifetime between the two. Slumped against a tree, he watched the sun's belly nudge the mountains on the horizon as the vibrant colors of soil and scrubland began to fade. There was maybe an hour of daylight left, and he knew nights around here fell cold and heavy.

Adam got up, brushed down his sweat-drenched summer clothes. *I need shelter, and fast.*

He was hiding out in one of the area's State Parks, surrounded now by miles and miles of plains and rock. He didn't know where he was. Hopefully, no one coming after him would know either.

The few people Adam had chanced upon were care-free hikers smiling as they passed. One guy even swallowed Adam's story about falling down a gully, and treated his scrapes properly with cotton wool and antiseptic. Better still, Adam had chanced upon a picnic site in the afternoon. He'd braved a trash bin full of wasps to feast on stale sandwich crusts and coffee dregs from paper cups.

"Dad always said I ate garbage," Adam murmured. "If he only knew. . . ."

Welcome to life on the run, he thought. *Oh, Dad, where are you?*

A line of cottonwood trees, their branches bristling with green arrowheads, dominated the valley below. Adam scrambled over the scrub toward them. He seemed to recall that these trees grew near water—and where you found water, you often found campsites. A stinky outhouse or a damp shower block was hardly a dream accommodation, but any cover was better than none. And maybe the bins there would offer a little late-night supper.

He was moving carefully through the gloomy valley, still racking his brains for some way out of this mess, when he heard a crack from the trees ahead. Adam froze. Wildlife or happy campers? He wasn't keen on running into either right now, so he crouched down behind a bush and waited to see what came out.

Within a minute he saw a tall, burly man emerge from the wood. No camper, then—the man wore a uniform shaded green and brown. A big shiny badge on his jacket caught the blood-orange light of sunset. A handgun hung from a holster at his side.

Park ranger? Adam felt sweat prickle his skin. Were they usually armed, or was this one looking for a dangerous fugitive . . . ?

A moment later he had his answer. Another ranger, massive and familiar, pushed out from the tree line a good twenty meters away. A vivid gash ran from his ear to the edge of his bushy mustache. Stitches clustered over the wound like flies feasting on the puckered flesh.

Adam held his breath and shrank deeper down into his scant cover. Bateman! What was he doing here?

"Pete's guys found forensics at a picnic site, east of the lake," Bateman announced. "Anything at that campground, Jonno?"

"Not a trace," the other man drawled back. "Maybe the kid's doubled back into town. Maybe he doesn't know he's wanted yet."

"He was seen running into the park. Something must've tipped him off." Bateman was looking all about. "He turned off his phone. Maybe he figured out it was bugged."

Adam frowned. He remembered Bateman holding his

phone, but had never suspected a thing; it had died of its own accord around lunchtime, the last juice drained from its batteries. Luckily for him.

"Think the kid's headed up into the mountains?" asked Jonno.

Bateman smirked. "Most likely he's got no clue where he's headed. He's one of those stay-at-home nerd types like his daddy. The Great Outdoors for them means the parking lot outside Blockbuster."

Adam bunched his fists. But at least they weren't talking about Dad in the past tense.

"This whole assignment stinks," Jonno declared. "If we can't find Adlar Junior ahead of you-know-what—"

"Aw, quit complaining." Bateman's fingertips strayed to his stitches. "You're like me—joined up with Geneflow 'cause tours in the Middle East weren't giving you the buzz no more." He clapped a hand on his friend's shoulder. "We've got grenades. Jam one of them down that thing's throat and it won't be taking out any more of us."

Jonno looked at him. "You really believe that after what happened this morning? The way that thing came back from the dead like a—"

"We were expecting to handle a kid." Bateman nodded slowly, looking all around. "This time, we'll be ready."

Disbelief and fear were crowding Adam's senses. How could he have got caught up in all this? *These people know you're here,* a part of him argued. *They're talking crud, trying to scare you into coming out.*

But even through the fronds that hid him, Adam could see fear in the men's eyes as they looked all around.

Who do I want to get me, he thought. *Them, or . . . it?*

Adam wished longingly for the power and poise of the glowering blond ninja of Ultra-Reality, the character he'd helped his dad develop. *Stomp kick and jab cross,* he thought, *take them down. . . .*

But, no—he was thirteen, sore, lost and way out of his depth.

Before he could even fully process the movement, his shaking legs were pushing him up out of cover. Both Jonno and Bateman turned at the sudden noise, drawing their handguns.

"Don't," Adam said hoarsely, hands raised in the air. "You got me."

"Son of a . . ." Jonno shook his head slowly. "The kid was right under our noses."

"Kid? Nah." Bateman's broad grin threatened to pop a stitch. "He's a dangerous criminal on the run. We've seen to that."

Adam fought to keep his voice steady. "Just take me to my dad."

Jonno's smile was as bogus as his ranger outfit. "Hear that, Frank? Kid thinks he can tell us what to do."

"I heard it." Bateman strode forward, grabbed hold

of Adam's arm and twisted it hard. Adam gasped in pain as the man forced him to his knees. "You little punk. Look at you—gutless as your old man. You had us by the short and curlies out here, and you go and give yourself up."

With a surge of anger, Adam tore his arm free and snatched for Bateman's gun. But Jonno jammed his revolver against Adam's temple. Adam heard the hammer cock with a bone-hard click. He froze statue-still, so scared he almost puked.

And then a great thumping crash from the nearby cottonwoods echoed through the valley.

Jonno jerked the gun away from Adam's head and toward the source of the sound. "What was that?"

"One guess," hissed Bateman, turning the same way. "Be ready with those grenades." He placed his boot in the small of Adam's back, forcing him belly-down in the grass. "All right," he shouted. "I know you can understand me, so hear this. We've got Adlar's boy. We believe you want him—and you can have him. But only if you come out slowly, and don't harm us."

"No!" Adam squirmed helplessly as Bateman's heel bit down harder against his spine.

"A bullet in the wrong place and the boy's no use to you." Bateman's voice was getting louder, hoarser. "I repeat, come out slowly or Adlar's kid is history. No tricks. . . ."

Suddenly the ground shook with fleet, pounding

footsteps—from just *behind* them. A bone-grinding roar almost tore Adam's ears off. The pressure vanished from his back as Bateman was sent hurtling through the air, arms flailing like he could fly. He couldn't. He crashed helplessly into the trees, out of sight.

At the same time, Jonno was screaming, a sound drenched with terror. Then the scream cut off with a crunching sound. An outstretched arm flopped down in front of Adam's face.

But the rest of the man was gone.

Adam felt the bile rise in his throat. Fear fixed him still where he lay. Then he saw Jonno's white-knuckled fingers were locked around the promised grenade. Saw that the pin had been pulled.

The next instant, a dark, scaly blur lashed out at the severed arm and batted it into the bushes. Adam gasped as he was snatched roughly from the ground as easily as a child might pick up a pinecone. He was locked into a vise of cold, reptilian flesh, pinned around the waist.

Then the colossal *thing* that had grabbed him bounded away through the darkening valley in huge leaps, as the grenade went off in a lightning-white flash.

7 ENCOUNTER

In the flare of the explosion, Adam realized the nightmare thing was no longer invisible. Frozen in a long moment of sheer, unbelieving terror, he saw it in gruesome glimpses.

He saw great knots of muscle dance and twitch as the monster ran. Teeth like carving knives, jutting from black and bloody jaws. The brute outline of a huge, reptilian head, like that on the screen in the library.

Adam squeezed his eyes closed. His ears still rang with the noise of the explosion. His heart was battering at his ribs. He felt as though he were dangling from the top-floor window of a speeding double-decker bus. His body felt scratched raw, his temples throbbed as he struggled for breath.

Then the valley vanished, replaced by complete darkness. It got suddenly colder. *We're in a cave,* Adam realized.

We're in this thing's lair.

He was dropped, surprisingly gently, to a floor of packed earth. It was black as tar in the cave; only a snatch of moonlight from outside filled the air. Heavy, hissing breaths filled the tunnel. Long claws clacked together, as if in anticipation of what they'd shred to ribbons next.

"Don't kill me," whispered Adam, rocking on his haunches, drenched with sweat. "You saved me out there. Please, please, don't kill me now. Please. . . ."

The monster loomed over him, thick ropes of drool stirring cold earth to mud as its jaws cranked open. . . .

"Please!" Adam begged as the mountainous creature leaned closer. "I . . . I don't know if you can understand my words but please, don't do this." He talked faster, speaking for his life. "I don't know why you came after me this morning or how you turned invisible. And I don't know why you want me now, but—"

A hard snout nudged up against Adam's ear. The warning rasp of the creature's breath was like sandpaper on his senses. Adam stopped talking, clamped his teeth down on his lower lip and tried to stop shaking. He was half grateful to the darkness for hiding most of this thing, yet terrified by the thought of what else might be lurking—

Something moved to his right.

"Keep away!" Adam said hoarsely.

"You're Adlar's kid, right?" It was a man's voice, calm and fragile from the shadows. "He found you then. After all we did to him, he could still find you."

"You know my dad?" Adam strained to see into the darkness. "What are you talking about? Who are you?"

"My name's Sedona, Mike Sedona. Zoologist."

"This thing came from a zoo?"

The creature gave a sharp snort of disgust. Adam felt the saliva hit his face. He spluttered, wiped his face on his sleeve as the thing lurched away from him. "Why's it taken us here?"

"This is where it came from," Sedona said distantly. "Fort Ponil."

Adam swallowed hard. "We're in Fort Ponil?"

"This cave hides the secret way in and out of the facility it was taught to use." The zoologist paused. "This time tomorrow, I would have been safe. Most of us have already cleared out. Relocated to Europe. I was going to follow. I would've—"

The shadowy shape growled menacingly. It sniffed the air as it padded about the cave—and suddenly, a fierce yellow glare spat from spotlights in the rocky ceiling. *Lights? Where did the lights come from?* Adam screwed up his eyes, blinked as his vision slowly adjusted.

Then, as the monster stood fully revealed at last, he wished they hadn't.

A dinosaur was glaring down at him.

A living, breathing, dark-green dinosaur. Like a T. rex. Adam's senses reeled. *That's all it can be,* he thought.

The paintings, the pictures and the movies, all the incredible special effects Adam had seen in his lifetime couldn't capture a fraction of the power and presence of the flesh-and-blood beast before him—this sleek and scaly juggernaut, watching him from under bloodred brows.

"It looks so real," Adam whispered. "But how . . . ?"

The sheer size of the thing was staggering. Its hind legs, each as big as a man, balanced its body in the middle—the broad trunk, neck and head hunching forward balanced the long tail tapering behind. Teeth like giant spikes and huge talons gleamed like horrific advertisements for the mauling tortures the monster could inflict. With a pang of alarm, Adam realized the arms and hands were different from the pictures he'd seen in the library—the limbs were longer, chunkier, more powerful, and each ended in a large hand with five clawed fingers, not the illustrated two. There were dark smears around the brutish face, like burn marks, that didn't make the monster look any prettier. But somehow the scariest things were its dark, beady eyes, gleaming with a cold intelligence.

Adam turned to Sedona—who turned out to be a black man with close-cropped hair, his white lab coat stained with dirt and blood. He was shivering, covered in sweat, clearly in shock. "A miracle of biology," he said. "Just look at him. Still standing after all we did. . . ."

"It was invisible before," Adam murmured, unable to tear his eyes away. "How . . . ?"

"Adaptive camouflage," Sedona hissed back. "It hunts by stealth. Skin like a chameleon's, only a billion times more sensitive. It secretes a substance that affects light rays, so that—" He broke off and screamed as the dinosaur stamped forward and grabbed him with one hand.

The next moment, Adam was grabbed too, and lifted roughly into the air. The monster turned with some difficulty in the narrow space, then bore them both away with a strange, almost birdlike gait, moving on tiptoes. The tunnel was studded with more spotlights, and Adam glimpsed the gory remains of something else in a lab coat, half crushed into the ground. He looked away, trying not to be sick.

The journey didn't last long, as the creature came to a halt beside an impressive metal doorway. Its five claws tapped a staccato rhythm on the keypad with impressive precision, and with a rumbling shake, the slab of steel ground opened onto darkness. *Where are we going?* Adam thought. But as the dinosaur tramped into the shadows, overhead lighting flickered on—and he felt his jaw drop for what had to be the fiftieth time that day.

The dinosaur had carried them into a freaky-looking high-tech laboratory carved out of a giant cave. The walls were rocky but lined with computers and cabinets and all kinds of incredible machines and medical tools. Colorful charts, maps and X-rays dangled down like decorations. A formidable-looking steel structure stood in the center of the room, like a giant caravan crossed with a tank. It was marked CONTAINMENT CHAMBER—although the meter-thick metal door hanging drunkenly from a single hinge suggested it hadn't lived up to its name.

Adam was dropped to the ground, followed by Sedona a few seconds later—headfirst. They both lay there, panting for breath. The huge creature seemed to forget them, swinging its great, scorched head from side to side as if searching something out. It trod stealthily about the laboratory, colossal muscles rippling with every movement.

"He killed the others," Sedona said slowly, "everyone who stayed to shut things down, he took them apart. All except me."

That could explain why it didn't grab me straight after I got away in the truck this morning, Adam thought. *It had had things to take care of back here.*

"Why *not* me?" Sedona was still muttering to himself. "I don't know. There'll be a reason. He doesn't do anything without a reason."

"Reason?" Adam guessed the man was hanging on to sanity by threads. "You make it sound like it's intelligent."

"If he could still talk, he could tell you himself." Sedona giggled suddenly, though his eyes remained wide with fear. "Sounds like a joke, doesn't it? A talking dinosaur."

Adam stared at him. "It could *speak*?"

"Sure. Until we got orders to put twenty thousand volts through his brain." The scientist chewed on the end of his finger. "Did as we were told, figured he was finished. Shipped him out to Utah, dumped him in a reservoir. But somehow, he pulled through, got back out. Must have headed straight to your apartment." Sedona shook his head in admiration. "I don't know why I'm surprised. He once zeroed in on a deer let loose in a hundred square miles of state park." He looked at Adam. "Finding your place would be a breeze."

"But why would it come after me?" Adam whispered.

"Confused your scent with your dad's, perhaps." Sedona looked at Adam. "See, it was your dad who tricked him—and put that current through his head."

Adam stared at him, reeling. *"What?"*

The creature roared suddenly with such violence that Adam cringed and fell silent.

"He knows we're talking about him." Sedona was staring at the ground. "He's not some dumb animal. He's a Z. rex."

Adam frowned. "Don't you mean *T. rex*?"

Sedona turned to him, his eyes haunted. "I mean Z."

The dinosaur shook its huge head. It came closer, mouth swinging open, displaying way too many teeth. "Zed," it rumbled, a low, warning noise like timbers creaking, its cold dark eyes glinting with malice.

Adam swallowed hard. "No way. Come on! No freakin' way!"

Even Sedona looked up now in wondering terror. "He *can* still speak. . . ."

"Zed," the creature rasped again. "Zed. Rex. Zed. REX."

8 ASSAULT

Adam watched the creature's scaly lips contorting to form the words. "This has got to be a trick," he said helplessly. "It's special effects, or—or *something*."

"I told you, he's a miracle of biology." Sedona was still gazing up at the dinosaur. "Z. rex, short for *Zenithsaurus rex*. Means, 'king of reptiles at his zenith.'"

"Zenith?"

"Highest point. The peak." Sedona shot Adam a look. "Your father called him Zed, not Zee like the rest of us. Seems the creature's picked up on that."

Dad switched his way of saying Z when he was teaching me the alphabet. . . . Adam shook his head, unable to take it all in. *You're stuck underground with a madman and a dinosaur,* his thoughts were screaming. *A dinosaur!* It was impossible to believe and yet just as impossible to deny.

There came a grating noise. "No . . ." The huge reptile was speaking again, staring down at Sedona, eyes narrowed and glaring. *"No . . ."*

"No . . . kill us?" Sedona said hopefully. "No keep us here? You're going to let us go?"

The Z. rex snorted with anger, turned and lurched away, resuming his hunt through the laboratory.

"Now, while he's distracted." Adam turned to the frightened scientist, his voice a hoarse whisper. "We can get out and close the door on him."

"He'd rip us apart before we were halfway across the room," said Sedona.

Adam didn't dare try anything alone. He watched the Z. rex, sick with fear. He knew that this thing could kill him in a dozen different ways. But it hadn't. Not so far. That had to be good, right? He kept telling himself that while the dinosaur turned over the lab as if hunting for something in particular.

"This is your dad's fault," Sedona muttered. "He screwed up."

"He works on computer games," Adam retorted. "Whatever he was made to do here, it was against his will."

"Oh, really?" Sedona laughed bitterly. "He was working happily enough every time I saw him."

"He can't have been." Adam put his head in his hands. "I don't get it, he was only here eight days—"

"ZED!" The blast of sound almost tore Adam's ears off, as the Z. rex strode over with a huge bundle of folders and clipboards and dumped them at his feet. "Zed . . . no." Cold reptile eyes glared down at him, one claw pointed accusingly at the mess of papers like it was somehow Adam's fault they'd been dropped. "No . . ." Scaly brows knotted in concentration, he tried one more time to get his lips around the word: "No . . . tes . . ."

"Notes!" Sedona cried suddenly. "You wanted me to find these notes for you? I'm sorry, I thought Josephs had shipped them out already."

"Notes," the reptile repeated more clearly, pointing at Adam.

"You . . . you want *me* to read this stuff?" Adam looked in dismay at equations and long Latin words and scientific jargon he couldn't even pronounce, let alone understand. "I—I can't. I don't get it. I'm thirteen, I'm still at school."

"This is a child, an immature human," said Sedona, jumping in quickly as if seeing an opportunity. "He . . . he lacks intelligence and skill. Whatever information you want out of these notes, I can help you. I can, I promise."

A low, grating sound formed in the monster's throat:

"Help . . . ?" He lashed out with his tail, and a metal vat buckled like wet cardboard, the sound reverberating around the lab. "HELP?"

"I'm just support staff!" Sedona screwed up his eyes and pressed his sweaty palms together. "It was Adlar who flicked the switch that hurt you, and Josephs who gave the order. Maybe . . . maybe I can help you find them?"

"No," hissed Adam.

"Geneflow Solutions has a base in the United Kingdom, in Edinburgh," Sedona babbled on. "If you'll let me go I can find an exact—"

The Z. rex stamped his foot down on the bundle of papers, stopping the scientist's rant short. As the echoes crashed on, he closed his scale-lidded eyes, his claws twitching dangerously. "Tell," came the sinister growl. "Tell. Zed."

"Tell you what?" Sedona whispered.

The creature shook his brutish head, pointed at the papers and then stared down at Adam. "Zed. *No . . .*"

"No?" Adam shrugged helplessly. "'Notes' again?"

Frustration creased the beast's forehead. "Tell. Zed."

"You mean"—Sedona looked uncertainly at Adam— "tell the kid *about* you?"

The dinosaur thing thrust his head closer to his prisoners, his breath coming in short, snarling snatches. Adam held very still, barely daring to breathe.

Sedona started babbling. "He was created here as a first step—the Z. rex, I mean. A first step toward changing the world." Sedona wiped his nose with the back of his hand. "He was Geneflow's emblem in a way. A synthesis of science and history, re-engineering the past—"

"If I'm supposed to understand this stuff, you're gonna have to go slow," Adam broke in, tensely. "What *is* Geneflow Solutions? Solutions for what?"

But then the reptile's huge nostrils, each the size of Adam's head, flared and twitched. Clearly agitated, he looked past them to the doorway and bared his teeth.

"Hold still, all of you!" came a shout from just outside.

"Bateman?" Hope flared suddenly in Sedona's dark eyes. "Bateman, I'm here!"

Adam's insides felt like mince in a grinder. *Some rescue*, he thought grimly, as three men wearing white armored hazard-suits and gas masks spilled inside through the doorway, packing strange, chunky handguns. *And some choice—the psycho ringmaster or his hungry lion*. The biggest man—and judging by the paunch, it was Bateman—stepped forward, his left arm clearly injured and strapped to his chest. Two more men appeared behind the others and guarded the doorway, wielding what looked to be rocket launchers.

The Z. rex roared defiantly. But the men held their ground.

Bateman pulled off his mask with his good arm. His heavyset face was swollen and bruised, and he looked even more like a once-great soldier gone to seed. "Sedona, take the kid and stand clear of that freak."

Obediently, Sedona tried to grab Adam by the arm.

"Get off me!" Adam pulled free and backed away from both the dinosaur and the new arrivals. He didn't know what to do, but he was sick of being pushed around.

"I'm sorry about before, kid," Bateman told him. "C'mon, I wouldn't really hurt you. . . ." He kept his eyes on the Z. rex. "Besides, you really want to be left alone with our friendly monster? Looks like it's got plans for you, kid. And you saw what it did to Jonno. . . ."

Adam shuddered as the reptile made a sound uncomfortably like laughter.

The noise sent Sedona backing away toward Bateman. "It killed Neil too, and Laura and Goldblum and—"

"Guess I got lucky," Bateman interrupted. "When it whacked me, I hit more bushes than trees." He waved his weapon. "I told you, my friends were patrolling the park with me, kid. This time we're prepared. That thing's not attacking, 'cause he knows what these guns can do to him. We can get you away, protect you."

"That thing" was looking at Adam now as if daring him to believe it.

"He means what he says, Adam," Sedona spoke up,

sounding more confident now. "Mr. Bateman is head of security, the best. The Z. rex could find his way back to Fort Ponil because he was spawned here. But I developed an antipheromone spray that deadens our scent so the creature can't sniff us out."

"That's how we could sneak up on it," Bateman added quietly, his weapon pointing at the dinosaur's head, his fat finger poised on the trigger. "And how the only trace of yer dad it could find was at his old apartment. We *can* hide you, Adam. We can take you to your dad—he's waiting for you back home in Edinburgh. And he's just dying to see you—"

That settled it. Bateman didn't inspire much trust, but right now . . .

I just want to see you again, Dad.

Slowly, carefully, Adam took a step toward Bateman.

The Z. rex bellowed with fury and swiped his tail into Adam's chest. Adam felt like he'd been smacked with a telephone pole. He flew through the air and landed on a workstation, knocking the PC and keyboard from the desk. As he gasped for breath, the air thumped from his lungs, he saw the dinosaur shimmer and all but disappear.

"How . . . ?" Adam breathed.

"Don't think so, dino-freak!" Bateman yelled, as he leveled his gun at the Z. rex and yanked on the trigger. A bolt of blazing blue energy tore from the barrel, soon joined by two more as the other men opened fire.

Electroshock weapons, like crazy, sci-fi shock-guns. Adam guessed—set to the highest possible voltage. The giant reptile became visible again, engulfed in a swell of crackling indigo, bellowing in pain and rage.

"Get him!" Sedona shrieked. "Get him, get him, get him!"

Adam watched the dinosaur's gruesome dance, revolted. This was his chance to run over to Bateman and the others, to try to split. But the creature was twisting and jerking this way and that in the flow of power.

Still blasting away, Bateman dropped to one knee, and his two buddies did the same—giving the men with the rocket launchers a clear aim at the struggling animal. . . .

But the Z. rex somehow caught an overturned swivel chair with the tip of his tail and propelled it across the floor toward Bateman. It slammed straight into the burly man, knocking the gun from his grip and sending him crashing into some lockers with a shout of pain. Sedona ran over to help him.

Now the reptile had only two blasts of current to contend with. Roaring his defiance, fighting against the powerful charge, he picked up the vat he'd already dented and brought it down on the two men. The sickening ring of steel on bone resonated around the room. Weapons and bodies crunched into the floor. The guns cut off dead.

The monster was free, and mad as all hell.

Even as the gunmen went down—and as Sedona tried desperately to revive Bateman—the guards in the doorway aimed their rocket launchers and prepared to open fire. Adam's blood ran cold as the Z. rex lunged forward, kicked one man aside with a huge, green foot and jabbed *left-right* at the other with his clawed fists, cracking ribs and body armor.

Stomp kick and jab cross. There was no mistaking the distinctive actions.

"My moves," Adam realized, as the world seemed to tilt in a violent, headlong rush. "That monster just used the moves *I* thought up for the Ultra-Reality demo. Which means . . ."

Dad did this. Adam clutched his temples. *Dad did this, Dad did this, Dad did—*

"NO!" Adam screamed.

The Z. rex turned from the bodies at his feet, his black, bright eyes fixing on Adam.

While the monster was distracted, Sedona left Bateman groaning beside the locker and scrabbled on the floor for an abandoned rocket launcher. "You're not killing anyone else!" he shouted.

The Z. rex swung around. Its lethal tail lashed out and caught Sedona under the chin. The scientist's neck snapped as his head twisted around one hundred eighty degrees, eyes turned to the door behind him, as if he were considering one final escape plan.

Then Sedona pitched to the floor, dead.

Adam stood very still, trying not to shake as, with a defiant growl, the Z. rex keeled over, apparently exhausted.

At the same moment, Bateman pulled out a stubby metal canister from a pocket in his hazard-suit and hurled it down on the floor with a clatter. Thick white mist started hissing from inside.

Oh, no way, thought Adam, new horror cutting blade-like through his thoughts. *Gas!*

9 DEPAR TURE

As the white gas began to fill the room, the Z. rex got back on his feet and a deep, crunching sound ripped through the air. Adam stared as the dinosaur's back split open, revealing something dark and ridged underneath. The next moment, two huge, spiny sails of gnarled flesh unfolded, impossibly outward. . . .

"Wings," Adam breathed in utter disbelief. "You're a dinosaur . . . and you've got *wings*!"

Wings that the Z. rex now flapped, and a strong wind blew up, tearing the gas haze apart like invisible teeth. Charts and papers pinned to the wall were snatched into the vortex. The backdraft knocked Adam to the ground.

And in the middle of the homemade tornado, the Z. rex rose up into the air like some monstrous dragon of legend. He reached down with his muscular arms, upturned the buckled metal vat and then dropped it over the gas canister.

The clang and clatter jarred Adam from just watching; he stepped over Sedona's body, ran through the white haze to the nearest of the two sprawled gunmen and clawed off a gas mask. He struggled into it and breathed again—sour, rank breaths but at least they were clearing his head.

"Mr. Bateman!" Adam shouted, staring all around, his voice muffled by the mask. "Where are you?" *My best hope is a man who's almost shot and gassed me,* he thought miserably. He staggered through the fumes toward the broken bodies in the doorway. But there was no sign of the stocky survivor. Bateman must've run for it.

Which means, I'm left all alone with—

A wet clacking sound made Adam turn. The dinosaur's incredible wings were folding up, disappearing into the thick ridges of scale and skin on his back. The Z. rex lowered his head and came stomping toward him once again.

"No!" Adam yelled, cowering on the floor. "Please!"

The monster scooped up Adam in his claws and thundered out through the doorway into the tunnel beyond. Adam clung grimly to the cold, muscular arm as though it were the restraint bar on a roller-coaster ride. He couldn't believe that he had already survived so much violence. Where was this going to end?

Dad really did put this thing into the Ultra-Reality game. The realization kept biting at Adam, the dinosaur's stomp kick and jab cross—and its aftermath—looping through his head in an endless action replay. Where else could the Z. rex have got those distinctive moves? *But the Think-Send tech was modeled on my brain waves. The game wouldn't work at all with anyone else playing it, Dad said so. . . .*

How could his father be a part of this madness?

The creature's step quickened, as if some scent were growing surer in his nostrils. As he rounded the corner, Adam saw a circle of night sky ahead, the way back out into the valley. Freedom. He pulled off his respirator. The air was almost painfully fresh after the atmosphere in the complex. Now, if he could only get away from this mad monster. . . .

Suddenly the Z. rex stopped dead, jarring Adam's bones. It cocked its massive, blackened head to one side.

"What . . . what is it?" Adam asked nervously.

The monster's only answer was to dump him on the ground and tread stealthily toward the exit, as if advancing on something invisible to Adam's eyes. Carefully, he crouched down, sniffed the air, then pulled away a loose tangle of gorse from beside the cave exit.

Adam crept up behind the dinosaur, wondering if he dared risk squeezing past and escaping into the park. If he could only find Bateman, then maybe—

The beast gave a growl of warning. There was no mistaking the message—"keep back." And as Adam peered past his captor's enormous leg, he realized why.

A digital clock face glowed cold blue from the shadows. It was fixed in place with wires on top of a small white bundle.

"A bomb?" Adam breathed, the words choking in his windpipe. *A big one too, if it's meant to wipe out a dinosaur.* "We've got to get out of here." He tried to speak in a low, firm voice, the way he'd seen people on TV talking to wild dogs, but to his own ears his words sounded shrill and feeble. "Look, if you can really understand, at least let *me* get out of here—"

With an impatient roar, the Z. rex used his tail to push Adam away, back down the tunnel toward the lab. Adam hesitated. *Run back to the lab,* he thought. *Hide under a desk. Hope the blast kills that thing, then you can get away.*

But as he was about to go, the massive reptile gave a hiss of satisfaction, turned and took a step toward him, flexing its claws. In one hand it was holding the bomb.

"No!" Adam staggered back, came up sharp against the rock wall. "Don't bring it inside!"

Ignoring him, the creature came closer.

"Outside!" Adam yelled. "Throw it outside, quick, it's going to—"

Then he saw that the clock face wasn't blinking. The countdown had stopped.

Adam clutched his chest and sank down against the wall. "It's okay. It's okay. Bateman must have mucked up when he set it."

There was a contemptuous look in the cold, black eyes. "Not man," the dinosaur ground out in that deep, raw-throated rasp. "Zed."

"You?" Adam looked at him uncertainly. *He thinks he defused it*.

Zed placed the bomb carefully on the ground, then grabbed Adam's arm and half pulled him, half carried him back down toward the laboratory. Adam gasped with pain, dangling like a doll in the dinosaur's grip— until he was dropped just inside the doorway and pushed roughly toward the scattered files.

"I already told you," Adam panted, massaging his bruised arm. "I can't read them."

The dinosaur watched him, eyes cold and bright.

Unable to meet that gaze, Adam crouched down and submissively started to tidy the files. "I—I'm sorry I tried to go with Bateman," he said shakily. "I'm just scared. Can't you see that? I lost my dad, my home, everything." He fell to his knees. "Please let me go. I can't help you, I don't know anything—"

"Know," Zed echoed. Or was he saying "No"? He was leaning over one of the dead men in the hazard-suits, opening up the rubber outfit from neck to waist with the tip of one gleaming claw. With surprising deftness, he pulled it free of the corpse. Then, with the fabric clamped in one hand, Zed crossed to a small fridge in one corner and tore off the door. He upended it, and a pile of drink cans and ready meals fell out noisily.

"Uh. . . ." Adam licked his dry lips. "You hungry?"

"You . . . hungry," Zed repeated, though as he rumbled through the syllables he made it sound more like a statement of fact. "Hungry. Need. Go."

Adam was baffled. "I . . . I'm sorry, I don't get you."

The monstrous creature hurled the hazard-suit at Adam's feet and pointed to it.

"What do I do with that? Wear it?" Adam looked doubtfully at the heap of white rubber. "I think it's kind of ruined."

"Need. Go."

Skin crawling, Adam climbed into the dead man's suit. He put on both legs, but before he could slip on the arms, Zed grunted and shook his head. He stretched out his tail and pointed to a map of the world on the wall.

The scaly tip hovered like an arrow over Scotland.

"Uh, yeah. Looks like everyone's either there or headed that way." Adam sighed. "If only *I* could get back too."

"Zed. Get. Back."

"What?" Adam shook his head, tired, scared and frustrated. "I don't know what you're saying."

With a wet crunching sound, Zed's sail-like wings unfolded again from his back. He looked at Adam, an unspoken challenge in his black crocodile eyes.

"What?" Adam shook his head. "You can't fly there."

"You," rasped the dinosaur. "Zed. Go."

"No." Adam felt his stomach twist. "No, you can't take me with you. Not all that way."

Zed kicked the empty fridge into the wall and stabbed a claw down at the jumble of food. "Hungry," he grunted. "Need. GO."

o   o   o

Thirty minutes later, Adam's stomach was full, but he felt sicker than ever. While he'd been eating, Zed had quietly, methodically gathered supplies in a couple of rucksacks: tins of food, matches, coats and blankets— and a selection of the mysterious files. Then the monster had fastened both bags to his tail.

His brain's been fried, Adam realized, still half dressed in the oversized hazard-suit. *He's been inside Ultra-Reality, and now he thinks life is like a video game, thinks he's a superhero. He reckons he can fly halfway across the world with me on his back.*

I have to run for it, he thought.

Then he pictured again what had happened to Sedona, and imagined how far he'd get.

In the end, Zed settled the matter. He grabbed Adam in both claws and thrust him upward onto his back. Terrified, Adam clung to a knobbly ridge on the dinosaur's back and managed to swing one leg over like a jockey, perching just above Zed's wings. Then Zed reached back, grabbed the flopping arms of the hazard-suit and used nimble claws to tie them tightly around his broad, scaly throat. That had the effect of securing Adam in a kind of makeshift harness, his body pressed up against the back of Zed's long neck as he clung on for dear life.

"I'm so gonna die," Adam moaned to himself.

The two rucksacks scraped and bounced over the rocky ground as Zed strode back toward the cave mouth.

"Don't you understand?" Adam shouted. "You can't do this! You're gonna kill us both!" The bomb still lay close to the entrance—and it seemed Adam would be proved right sooner than he'd thought as Zed stooped, picked up the explosives and studied them carefully.

"Zed . . . please put that down," Adam begged him, hearing the scratch of claws against wires. "Please, *please* put it down before you—"

The bomb made an ominous, electronic belch, and the blue numbers glowed back into being. There were now thirty seconds clicking down on the display.

"Get rid of it!" Adam almost sobbed. "C'mon, you can't know what you're doing. . . ."

Zed calmly placed the bundle down beside the entrance and strode out into the cold night darkness. His wings unfurled like broad sails, lifted to the rising wind. Then Adam gasped and gripped on as, with a sickening lurch, his unlikely mount launched skyward. *Hold on,* he willed himself. *Hold on as hard as you can*. The world tumbled and spun about him as they climbed up into the starry blackness. The wind teased tears from his eyes as they went higher, higher over the crumpled shadows of the wilderness park.

The bomb detonated with a roiling bloom of fire. The deafening boom of the blast left Adam's ears screaming and his heart in his mouth, as the explosion consumed rock, soil and air with the same greed and vigor. Adam saw the entrance to the abandoned lab collapse, entombed beneath tons of rubble.

Then he did *know what he was doing,* Adam realized.

Just what are you, Zed?

The skull-like moon watched balefully as Adam was swept away from the heat and the light on the dinosaur's back, deeper and deeper into the cold, star-scattered darkness.

10 FLIGHT

I'm *getting used to feeling scared. It's not so bad.*

So Adam had been telling himself, over and over. But hurtling through the skies, clinging to the back of an impossible flesh-eating monster, he knew the lie for the total garbage it was. Each flight was terrifying, from the first lurching takeoff to the final jarring touchdown.

It turned out that Zed could fly incredibly fast over extraordinary distances. But such progress came at a cost. Within minutes of being airborne, Adam would lose all feeling in his face and fingers as the night wind whipped against his skin. His perch on the monster's back felt precarious at best, but with the high altitudes robbing him of breath, his head kept spinning, and waves of nausea rolled through him. It was like being trapped on the world's most evil roller coaster for hours at a time with only a big elastic band holding you on board.

Even so, he didn't dare complain too loudly. There was no one to listen except Zed, who was doing all the real work, flapping those incredible wings of his hour after hour. It seemed the plan was to rest by day and fly by night so as not to be seen; clearly, not even a Z. rex could stay invisible for hours at a time while flying at ridiculous speeds.

Adam soon discovered that even intense fear couldn't hold off boredom indefinitely. With no one to talk to, he felt as if he were going quietly crazy. He worried about his dad, thought about his friends, about the way their numbers and texts were stored inside his dead phone. A little electronic tomb that held the remnants of his old, predictable life, meaningless in this new one.

o   o   o

After the second night's flying, they camped out beside an enormous lake as the dawn rose.

Adam rested on the deserted beach, sore, sour and shivering, watching Zed as he built a rocky shelter next to a hillside. The dinosaur worked quickly, shifting boulders with his brawny arms and adjusting their position with his jaws. It was clearly no casual arrangement. Zed layered the stones with mud and brushwood and kept crawling in and out, as though he were testing his shelter not just for cover but for camouflage too.

He doesn't want to be spotted while he sleeps, Adam realized. Vaguely he wondered how far he might run before the dinosaur woke up and came looking for him—and what punishments he might receive. He felt completely helpless. Even if he found other people nearby who might help him escape, what good would it do? Zed could kill them all, just as he'd killed Bateman's "friends."

Adam curled up on the grass and drifted into an exhausted sleep.

o o o

Around midday, Adam woke with a start to find Zed emerging from his hideaway, scenting the air. Stealthily, the dinosaur padded toward the beach, shimmering into invisibility as he went.

Adam watched in uneasy wonder. If he squinted he could make out the faint edges of Zed's form ghosting in the sunlight, but only because he knew what he was looking for. And he saw that the dinosaur was stalking toward a group of large, dark cormorants. "Like a stealth fighter closing on its target," Adam muttered. The birds shifted about uncertainly, as if sensing some kind of danger, but not its direction.

Then suddenly Zed snapped back into view, jaws

lunging, tail swiping, huge claws raking the air with deadly precision. A few of the large birds clattered away, escaping over water. Most were not so lucky. Shaken, Adam could see about a dozen dead or injured on the shore. One by one they vanished into Zed's jaws, swallowed whole.

The dinosaur smoothed out the bloody, churned-up sand with one massive foot, then turned and retreated to his shelter without a glance at his unwilling companion.

o o o

Aching too much to sleep any longer, Adam passed the afternoon gathering sticks and tinder in the hope of starting a fire. Then he started searching for matches in one of the rucksacks. He found instead the mysterious files Zed had collected and packed carefully at the bottom.

Why had Zed wanted Sedona to explain those files to Adam? If only Bateman hadn't turned up when he did, Adam guessed he'd know a lot more about whatever mad, mutant experiment had been going on at Ponil— and how his dad figured in things. Instead . . .

He shook his head to clear the horrible memories. "Where *are* the stupid matches?"

As if at the sound of Adam's voice, Zed crawled out from his shelter. Adam backed away as the dinosaur approached his pile of dry grass and sticks, watched as the giant creature struck his massive claws against a rock and set great sparks jumping. As the tinder started to smoke, Zed carefully pursed his lips and blew gently enough not to scatter the kindling. The fire was blazing in moments.

A regular Boy Scout, Adam thought wryly. He shuffled closer to the flames, but they couldn't seem to touch the coldness inside him. *How does Zed know stuff like this? Dinosaurs never made fire. . . .* He caught himself. Of course, dinosaurs had never performed kickboxing routines they picked up from a video game either. Or talked. And since when had they defused bombs?

Adam bit his lip. The truth of that night had been flickering at the back of his mind. It wasn't Bateman who had loused up at all. Zed had defused the bomb and then set it off after they left so Bateman would think it had worked after all . . . that he and Zed were dead and buried inside.

He stared in awe at the dinosaur beside him. "You're a devious wee monster, aren't you?"

Zed made no response, staring at the fire as if transfixed by his creation.

Yeah, devious. Clever. A killer.

And edging closer to civilization.

Wearily, Adam reached into one of the rucksack's side pockets and unfolded the map of the world that

Zed had torn down from the wall. "Wonder where we are now?"

Abruptly, Zed leaned forward and stretched out an arm toward him. Adam flinched as the point of the dinosaur's index claw tapped down on the map with precision.

"Ontario?" Adam read, as Zed retreated to his original position. "How would you know that? I mean . . . are you navigating by the stars? You can't come with built-in sat-nav. . . ." He shook his head. "Where did you *come* from?"

The dinosaur seemed not to hear. His dark eyes were fixed on the fire once more, reflecting the flames' pattern and dance.

o   o   o

That night, Adam decided to wear the gas mask he'd packed, to ward off the chill and keep the sting of the wind from his eyes. But it did little to improve his comfort, and the rubbery smell didn't help his nausea any.

He rested his cheek against Zed's neck. Even through the rubber, Adam could feel the dinosaur's knots of muscle bunch and relax with every sweep of those powerful wings. He closed his eyes, wished he could sleep and wake to find the journey was over. Or better, that this whole nightmare had been exactly that—a bad dream. Maybe he'd had a fever or something, and would wake to find his dad smiling down at him. "Quite a temperature you had there, Ad, but now it's—"

Falling.

Adam jerked awake to find himself in free fall, tumbling through the night, arms and legs windmilling helplessly. For a dizzying moment he couldn't tell up from down or ground from sky. The sleeves of the hazard-suit flapped uselessly around him in the fierce gale of his descent; the knots Zed had tied in them must have come loose.

He screamed through his mask, a raw shriek of horror.

Buffeted by the wind, turning in midair, Adam saw a dark shadow rushing up to meet him and braced himself for the impact. But the next moment, hard pressure clamped down on his rib cage. His body jerked—and suddenly he was lifted upward in the rough grip of two massive claws. The sprawling shadow was above him, all but swamping the stars as its huge wings beat violently through the night.

Adam felt sick with shock and relief. The killer dinosaur had just saved his life.

Sure he saved you, a mocking voice said. *He's not taking you on this little trip for nothing.*

He's got plans, and he needs you in one piece. For now.

o o o

By the time dawn had begun to bleed away the blackness of night, Adam could spare no thoughts for the beauty or the wonder of the sunrise over the Adirondack mountains, only a searing sense of gratitude that the ordeal would soon be over for a few more hours.

Zed touched down beside a fast-flowing creek that trailed through a rocky valley like so much black ribbon. He and Adam crashed out in the shelter of the sheer mountainside.

Adam refilled the empty water bottles from the stream. He had never felt more exhausted. His ribs were bruised mud-black. Every movement hurt him and his muscles felt ready to peel away from his bones. And his thoughts kept jerking back to his free-fall flight. The way Zed had swooped down and snatched him from certain death.

He glanced across at the dinosaur, who lay curled up on his side, his wings tightly folded under his bony back. "I thought I was dead last night," Adam told him. "That was quite a move you pulled off."

Zed didn't react, his breathing shallow, black eyes dull.

"Guess I should say thanks, huh?" Adam screwed the cap onto one of the refilled bottles and snorted softly. "Yeah. Thanks to my dad. Thanks for dragging me into this whole stupid situation." He shook his head miserably, flapped the stretched, grimy sleeves of the hazard-suit. "Oh, Dad—"

"Dad," Zed rasped suddenly. "W . . . X . . . Y . . . Z."

Adam looked at him warily. "What's the alphabet got to do with anything?"

The creature tried again. "Y . . . zed."

"Yeah. Dad changed the way he said it, thought I might get confused. Must've thought I was stupid."

Zed went on muttering in his hoarse sandpaper voice. "Y . . . Z."

Adam looked at his disheveled reflection in the water of the creek. "Why *me*?" he whispered.

o o o

To Adam, the flight from the Adirondacks to Newfoundland felt like the longest yet, through driving rain and gusting wind. The heavens decided to put on a light show, with toothy forks of lightning zigzagging past over the forests of Maine. Thunder ripped all around. The clouds were like giant, black timbers stacked in front of the stars.

Adam had hurtled on through it all, hunched up on Zed's back as those wings doggedly knifed at the rain-lashed night.

Now here he was with dusk tugging down the shutters on the fourth day, perched on a desolate crag that stuck out from the churning Atlantic like a bad tooth, staring out to sea. The sun was finally shining, but Adam still felt cold, damp and rotten.

Zed had hardly stirred all day, except to go shark fishing around noon. He had an unusual technique. First, he scraped a daggered claw along his muscular forearm. Then he plunged the bleeding flesh into the sea, and stood waiting, motionless and alert, for as long as it took.

Adam shuddered to remember the sight of Zed snatching his arm from the sea with an enormous shark hanging from the end of it. It had flapped about in a frenzy, refusing to relinquish its scaly catch even as it vanished down inside Zed's bulging throat like an olive sucked from a cocktail stick. A minute or so later, Zed spat out some bloody lumps back into the water—and so attracted more sharks.

It was typical of the dinosaur's strategies, Adam decided—intelligent, brutal and entirely successful.

"My stomach's grown a lot stronger since I met you," Adam reflected, watching the resting goliath. He supposed that the fact he was able to make jokes about stuff must prove he was getting used to Zed's existence. Then again, it was tricky to go on disbelieving when you were hog-tied to the evidence, night after night.

But it was one thing to accept the existence of talking, flying dinosaurs, another to have to sit so close to those giant jaws, to have those black, unblinking eyes fixed on you hungrily.

They stood on their tiny pinnacle of rock together, prisoner and jailer.

"How're you feeling, Zed?" Adam said suddenly. "Those burns on your face look like they're getting better."

The creature didn't react. Adam persisted, craving some kind of acknowledgment. "I ache everywhere. But I'm sort of getting used to it." He noticed a thick trickle of crimson running freely from the shark bites on Zed's arm. "Hey, you're still bleeding from earlier. Doesn't it hurt?"

Zed regarded him, suspicion in his eyes.

Adam wondered if here was a possible way to get the animal on his side. "We should maybe try to bandage that cut. It could get infected." He rummaged in one of the rucksacks for the small navy sweater he'd been using for a towel and pillow. "I could use this to stop the bleeding."

As he held up the sweater, the dinosaur growled in warning. Adam was about to back down, but knew an opportunity like this might not come again. If he could only win the creature's trust, prove that he had some usefulness over and above whatever Zed had planned for him . . . if he could make this thing start to think of him as a *friend*. . . .

"You saved me before," Adam said quietly. "Let me help you now."

The dinosaur shifted uncertainly, bared his teeth. Adam's legs started to tremble. *Come on,* he told himself, *you've been crushed up against him for the last who-knows-how-long. He hasn't eaten you yet.*

Yeah, but you weren't walking right into his jaws like this before.

Holding his breath, fumbling like an idiot, he placed the sweater around the beast's gory arm as gently as he could. Again, Zed made that low warning rattle in the back of his throat. Trying not to whimper, Adam tied the sleeves of the sweater in a crude knot and backed hurriedly away.

Zed stared down blankly at the dark woolen accessory he had just acquired. Adam bit his lip as an unexpected smile twitched at his cheeks. It looked as though the dinosaur was wearing a big blue bow.

"There we go," Adam murmured, turning to hide his amusement. "Much better." He reached into one of the rucksacks and pulled out the crumpled map. "Wonder where we are now?"

Zed reached over with his bandaged arm and gestured to somewhere around Newfoundland.

"Really? So, only about twenty-five hundred miles of Atlantic Ocean between us and dry land, then." Adam closed his eyes, lacking the will even to summon a hysterical laugh. "We'll hit Ireland first. Little hop from there, and we're home. Easy." He blew out a long sigh. "Still, I guess we can fly by day as well, now—there'll be no one below to see us. If you're up to it, I mean.

And if we can survive on a gallon of fresh water between us . . ."

Adam trailed off as Zed turned from him, batting
one loose arm of the sweater bandage like an overgrown kitten playing with wool.

"If we do get to Scotland," Adam began again, "you'll
be going after the people who hurt you, right? To go so
far, you've got to be." He took a deep breath. "Just remember, my dad was only at Fort Ponil for eight days.
He was forced to work there." *Just like you're forcing me
to stay with you,* he thought. "He would never have
wanted to hurt you, Zed. They made him do it."

Zed lay down and stared out over the water. "No,"
he growled.

"Yes!" Adam insisted. "And so I want to get back at
them too, Zed. Geneflow Solutions has messed up everything in my life. I don't know what you want from me,
but if I can help you get back at them, I will."

This time, the huge reptile made no reply.

"You must be so tired," Adam went on nervously.
"I mean, to put yourself through this kind of strain,
night after night . . . how do you do it?" He hesitated, as curiosity got the better of fear. "It's almost as
if you were made for this kind of life. What *were* you
made for?"

But Zed kept staring out over the horizon, and Adam's only answer was the foam and crash of the
dark sea.

11 HOMEC OMING

For Adam, the days that followed became a numbing blur of ocean and sky, of flight and fitful sleep. Adam dreamed of soft beds, hot food and as much cool water as he could drink.

As sunlight ebbed from the eighth long day, Adam watched land resolve itself slowly out of wreaths of low cloud. If they were on track, then this could be the west coast of Ireland. Adam felt a sense of growing excitement. He'd actually managed to live through this insane odyssey.

But any happiness was wiped out by growing nerves about what he was going to do when they got to Edinburgh.

Or rather, what Zed was going to do.

o   o   o

Finally, without fanfare, the long voyage ended a little after three the next morning.

As Zed powered toward the misty glow of the city lights, Adam ripped off his gas mask with numb fingers and hurled it away with a whoop of exhilaration. He stared down over the moonlit roofs and hills and spires of the home he'd thought he'd never see again and could have cried with relief.

Zed slowly descended over the dark wildness of Holyrood Park, that massive sprawl of hills, lochs and crags right in the center of the city. Though his mouth was sore and dry and his stomach growling like a grizzly, Adam's spirits rose ever higher the lower they flew.

"We did it!" he yelled. "Zed, you actually got us here! You can put us down there—that big mound thing. It's Arthur's Seat, an extinct volcano, super old. From there you can see out over the whole city. . . ."

Zed seemed to be heading for it already, regardless of Adam's recommendation. He landed heavily on a grassy slope with a grunt of pain and effort, and sank to the ground. Adam scrambled out of his hazard-suit harness and tumbled to the wet springy turf. He pressed his face against it, licking up the dew and muttering prayers of thanks to anyone who'd listen. "I never thought I'd get back in one piece. . . ."

He realized Zed had keeled over and was doing the same, desperately lapping at the dew-soaked grass. Somehow, with one wing folded and the other hanging limp by his side, the dinosaur looked not so much frightening as pitiful. How much water must a dinosaur need? Loads, surely. Adam felt a moment's fleeting guilt at draining the last of their supply the day before.

No, stuff that, he told himself. *I'm not feeling sorry for that thing after all he's put me through.*

Wiping his chapped lips, Adam scrambled up. He hurt just about everywhere, with some wicked pressure sores from clamping his legs around the dinosaur's back, but right now even the pain felt like his body celebrating its survival. It was fantastic feeling solid ground under his feet—ground that wasn't going to shift. And he reveled in the sight of the old familiar city skyline. Before him were the high-rise shoe-box shadows of the Pollock Halls, looming guardians of the straight lines and slopes of the estates beyond. He looked farther, to the floodlit castle standing massive on the mound and the ghostly edges of the rugged, indomitable city skyline. How many times had he stood here, untroubled, gazing out over it all?

And now he'd come in the company of a killer.

After spending more than a week up close and personal with a real-life mutant dinosaur, Adam realized he'd grown almost accustomed to Zed's huge, menacing presence. Almost. But now they stood in a small city of half a million people—during Festival month, no less. The streets would be overloaded with tourists and weirdos up for the Fringe—writers, filmmakers, people handing out flyers. . . .

Adam's euphoria fled. The ache began to twist through his bones again. *Yeah, whoopee, you made it,* he thought. *And now everyone you know, and masses more you don't . . . their lives could all be in danger.*

"Here"—a thick string of drool hung from the dinosaur's jaws as he sniffed the air—"Zed . . . again . . . here. . . ."

"You think you've been here before?" Adam raised his eyebrows. "I dunno how old you are, but maybe you have, maybe that's how you found your way straight to Arthur's Seat. Or maybe"—a thought struck him queasily—"you've picked up some of my moves from Dad's Ultra-Reality software. Since the Think-Send stuff was built around my brain waves, p'raps you picked up some of my memories too?" He looked at his scaly captor and heaved a sigh. "Whatever, we don't have long before the whole city starts waking up. So, what's next?"

Zed rose up, muscles and sinews twitching, his bulk blotting out the moon. He stretched out both wings, grabbed Adam roughly and slung him across his back.

"What?" Adam protested. "No, please, we just got here. I need to rest. You can't have found Geneflow already?"

"Not find," rasped Zed, his voice hoarse and raw. "Go."

And with a wild, sickening lurch, he went.

o   o   o

They flew across the city, Adam clinging to the dinosaur's knobbly back without his harness now, apprehension clouding his pain. He'd caught barely a snatch of the sandstone splendor of his home city, and now he was already leaving it behind. With moonlight stirring the dark soup of cloud and sky, Adam watched the estates drift past below; streets and houses laid out in intricate order like the circuit diagrams his dad used to pore over.

Zed seemed to be making for somewhere around Granton. *That's where I would have gone,* Adam decided. Developers were sinking a mint into doing up the waterfront area, but there were still plenty of vacant warehouses, abandoned factories and broken-down businesses. It would make a good place to hide out.

The streets grew scruffier, farther north. Browbeaten terraces of dark, rain-washed brick huddled next to stone yards, cement works and building sites. The vast skeleton of a gasometer yawned open below as if trying to engulf them. Parked cars and vans stood out bright against the asphalt, like mites in clusters feeding on dark branches.

After circling the area a few times, Zed descended

over a three-story crate of moldering gray brick with a wide, sloping roof. The warehouse bordered a stretch of wasteland on one side and the ramshackle yard of a decaying gasworks on the other, and it was big enough to hide a dozen dinosaurs. Those windows still intact were caked with filth. A large handwritten sign tied to the barbed wire topping a chain-link fence announced that the textiles business had moved premises to an address in West Lothian.

"Prepare for squatters," Adam muttered.

Zed dropped down over the fence and landed harder than usual to the side of the abandoned warehouse. Adam was jarred free from his perch, slipping down to land painfully on his back.

The giant reptile sliced through the ropes securing the rucksacks to his legs and stamped over to a large puddle where he lapped greedily at the water. Then he stalked back, bit through the heavy chain securing the fire doors and shoved them open. But Zed couldn't squeeze through—he was way too big. The sweater bandage on his forearm snagged on the rotting wooden doorframe. With an impatient snort, the dinosaur slashed the fabric in two and stomped away in search of another entrance.

Adam eyed the discarded sweater nervously. *That was meant to be a reminder of how useful I can be,* he thought. "There'll be delivery doors someplace," Adam called, grabbing the rucksacks and hurrying after him. "Big enough for you to get through."

But Zed had already found them, panting for breath in front of a wide, rusting roll-up door. It was drawn closed, of course, save for a narrow gap at the bottom. As the dinosaur crouched and gripped the lower edge of the shutter with his powerful claws, Adam noticed that the wounds beneath the bandage had already healed, vanished just like the burns on Zed's head. *No wonder you weren't killed when all that electricity was put through your brain,* he thought grimly.

And if we're here so Zed can get revenge, what part do I play?

"I could go inside and open the delivery doors for you," Adam suggested, desperate to try and keep the monster on his side. "If you force your way in, someone might notice the damage and call the police. Cause trouble."

Zed glared down at him for a few seconds. Then he hissed through his nostrils and took a step back.

Adam squeezed under the doorway and wriggled through into the old warehouse. It was dank and gloomy and stank of old, musty fabrics. Long, crumbling rolls of carpet lay in rotting piles against the damp brickwork. A sharp wind whistled through broken windows. Adam peered at some rusted chains beside the roll-up door and hauled on them hard. The mechanism was stiff with disuse, but he managed to get the door jerking upward, revealing Zed's bulk outside, bit by scary bit. The dinosaur kicked the rucksacks inside, then followed them, staring around at the damp and drafty hall. With a dismissive snort, he shuffled over to the rolls of ruined carpet and slumped down on top of them.

"No place like home." Adam shoved his hands in his pockets. "Hey, you sniffed out mine and Dad's apartment in New Mexico easily enough. Can you smell where we live here?"

Zed grunted. "Old smell."

"Okay, so Dad may not have been back. But if these Geneflow people use that antistink spray, you can't know *who* has gone there." Adam frowned. "Funny though. If they think you were blown up by that bomb, why would they still be using the spray? Unless it never wears off. . . ." He shrugged, swallowing hard. "Anyway. I should really go and check out my apartment. . . ."

Zed raised his brutish head, pronounced one word carefully and with menacing emphasis. "No."

"But we've got no water, no food, no cash for anything—"

"NO," the reptile rasped.

Adam felt frustration start to boil beneath his fear. "Look, I'm not sure why you've brought me here, but you've kept me alive so far. If you want me to stay that way and with all my marbles, there's stuff I need." *I'm arguing with a killer dinosaur,* he realized, and quickly softened his voice. "There's food, clothes and an emergency stash of money at my flat . . . and who knows, I might even find a clue there to where Dad's gone."

Zed's eyes narrowed and his jaws scissored open. "Dad. Dead. . . ." He rolled his tongue around the words, sharp and fast. "Dad. Dead."

Heart pounding in his chest, Adam shook his head. "What? Don't say that! You heard Bateman back at the lab—Dad's *not* dead. Anyway, Josephs needs him. He's been *forced* to work for these people. He sent a message to my phone, telling me to reach someone who could help to sort them out. . . ." He pulled out his phone. "You understand texting? If I can get a charger from my flat, I can show you the message and prove it to you. I don't have a key to get in, but—"

"Win." Zed stared at him and nodded slowly. "Win . . . dow."

Adam frowned. "I *did* once get in through my window for a dare. Nearly killed me." He felt a shiver pass through him. "Are you remembering that?"

The beast watched him silently.

"Look, I know running away won't do any good. You can find me anyplace. So how about if I promise to come straight back?" Adam sighed. "If you *can* remember stuff, you should know I keep a promise."

"Miss," echoed Zed. He wrapped his tail about his legs like a giant python, his eyelids starting to close. "Rem . . . ember."

Adam hovered uncertainly as the dinosaur's head slumped back, the great breaths settling into a rasping rhythm. He waited a few minutes, looking longingly over his shoulder at the exit where a few hours' freedom was waiting.

Finally he summoned all his nerve and walked outside. The dinosaur stayed sleeping. But the huge, misshapen clouds in the sky reminded him of Zed's nightmarish shadow, hanging over him still.

12 INTRUDER

Adam's apartment was three miles to the south, about an hour's walk back into town. The morning was cold and musty smelling, such a change from the dry heat of New Mexico. At first, despite his aching legs, he relished the space and quiet. He was free, just for a while. And he was home! He could call up his mates, surprise them, drag them out of bed. *"Guys, you won't believe what I've been through. . . ."*

But the old doubts and fears were soon biting at the back of his mind, and suddenly he felt more like a ghost than a returning hero. How could he risk involving his friends with kidnappers and killers—with monsters?

Lonely and troubled, Adam detoured toward the

heart of Edinburgh. After so long away from civilization, he was longing to feel a part of real life. So he made his way over to the Mound in the mizzling dawn light, the steep road that climbed over the railway line and the tent-studded greenness of Princes Street Gardens. The sky was slate-gray, as impassive and solid as the great blocks and spires of the antique buildings looming before him. Banks and galleries and soot-shod old buildings stood proudly about. Darkened pub windows eyed churches warily from across the street. It was quiet, with little traffic rumbling back and forth. To his right, lording over all the roofs and spires of the stern skyline was the Castle, perched on its huge craggy skirts of volcanic rock.

Adam looked up suddenly, his heart jolting as he glimpsed a dark blur in the sky overhead. *Zed's woken up,* he thought in a panic. *He's checking up on me.*

But his imagination was playing tricks. There was nothing there. Nothing he could see, at any rate.

After scanning the sky a little longer, Adam turned and trudged away back toward Princes Street and the grand sandstone streets of the New Town.

Finally he turned onto Northumberland Street, a spacious sweep of elegant Georgian houses. He felt his spirits brighten a little at the sight of his apartment. The heavy front door was painted fire-engine red, with a fan-shaped window above. Adam had always found it so cheery and welcoming. Now the triangles of glass in the fan looked like vicious fangs above a door covered in blood. With a shudder, Adam continued west along the street and took the next right to double back to the rear gardens. No one was about. He scrambled over a fence, looked up at his bedroom window and wondered if the drainpipe running up the wall would still bear his weight.

Only one way to find out, he decided.

The worn muscles in Adam's arms and legs protested as he started to climb. But Zed had traveled for thousands of miles; Adam wasn't going to let a few vertical meters get the better of him. With one arm gripping the drainpipe and the toes of both feet wedged against a fixing in the wall, he reached over to his bedroom window and wobbled the flat of his hand against the glass. It had never latched properly, and if he jiggled it in just the right way. . . .

"Got you," he whispered as he felt it start to shift upward. As soon as he judged the gap large enough, he lunged over the sill and pulled himself clumsily inside, collapsing onto the bed. *His* bed.

He closed his eyes, breathed in the familiar smells and clung to the soft mattress. If only he could sleep here properly for a few hours, to "wallow in his pit" as Dad used to say.

At the thought of his dad, Adam's eyes sprang open. He got up from the bed almost guiltily—and frowned.

His belongings were strewn all over the room, a

knotted landscape of comics, clothes and DVDs. *Burglars,* he thought. And yet the LCD television was still on the shelf. In a daze, he walked out into the bright magnolia hallway. His bike was still there, that was something—he wouldn't have to walk back to the warehouse, and could enjoy his time away for a little longer.

Adam checked his dad's room. It had been royally trashed too. Suddenly he remembered the way Bateman had gone searching through his father's room in New Mexico for something he hadn't found. Someone had tried the same thing here.

Angrily, Adam crossed to the phone in the hallway. It had been smashed along with the answering machine. The kitchen was a mess, all the dishes, pans and cutlery upended in the middle of the room. The coffee jar containing the emergency stash of cash lay empty.

He filled a chipped mug with water and drained it dry. Then he wandered around the apartment again, bone-weary and shell-shocked. *Well, what did you expect?* asked a voice somewhere inside. *This is your life, now—all messed up with the good stuff broken. Just grab a few bits and creep back to the monster and the old, cold building in the dark. What else are you going to do—give up and cry?*

He wiped his nose. The idea had some appeal, but no way was he caving in now. Not after coming so far.

He went to the bathroom and took a quick shower;

no time to wait for hot water, so it was cold but still welcome. Then he squeezed half a tube of toothpaste into his mouth and swilled it about with water from a tap—*God, what luxury!* Mouth tingling, he pressed an old roll-on deodorant into service, put on fresh clothes and strode into the living room. It was a mess, but hadn't been gone over as badly as the bedrooms.

Feeling a little more human now, Adam deliberated his next move. He decided the most important thing was to get Dad's message to Jeff Hayden, maybe try to smuggle out some of the files. Zed had wanted to share the story of his creation with Adam—he was sure Mr. Hayden would explain. . . .

He started to search for his dad's other phone— Mr. Adlar lost handsets so often he always kept a backup good to go. Jeff Hayden's contact details would surely be held on there. Adam found the battered old Nokia handset and its charger beneath a pile of scattered magazines. A double result—the charger would work for his phone too.

Then he suddenly remembered: back in the state park, Bateman had said Adam's phone was bugged. Would they be able to track him here too, and come to get him?

And if they did, and took him back to his dad . . . in some ways, wouldn't that be a relief?

Suddenly Adam found he wasn't sure. He pictured Zed waking up in that run-down warehouse, alone. Coming looking. What might the dinosaur do if Adam could not be found?

And what might his dad be forced to do, if Josephs and Bateman threatened Adam's life?

Leaving his phone on charge but safely switched off, he returned to his bedroom and grabbed his school sports bag. He stuffed his dad's headset, a sleeping bag, toiletries and fresh clothes inside. Then he collected some groceries from the back of the cupboard and shoved them into the bag along with a jacket, a flashlight, an alarm clock and an old bobble hat. On the floor, he saw a framed photo of him and his dad, smiling over ice creams. Amazingly, the glass in the frame hadn't cracked. He decided to pack that too. If only the cash hadn't been taken—

Suddenly, Adam remembered his old piggy bank. He'd kept it hidden in the drawer under his bed ever since his mate Kevin had teased him about it, saying it was babyish. Perhaps it had escaped discovery.

It was just as he crouched down to see that he looked over and saw the broken length of thread trailing from the windowsill.

His blood ran cold. The thread must have pulled tight and snapped as he'd clambered through the window, triggering . . . what?

Holding his breath, Adam followed the thread to a tiny electronic device screwed to the underside of the sill. It was too small for a bomb, surely—and why hadn't it gone off as soon as he'd entered? Maybe it was broken?

A signaling device, he realized. *Whoever planted it knew the bedroom window was someone's best bet for getting in.*

And now I've set it off, and they know I'm here.

With fumbling fingers, he grabbed the piggy bank and jammed it into the sports bag. Then he unplugged the charger and his phone and stuffed them in after it. He swung the bag onto his shoulder, grabbed his bike and wheeled it out of the apartment. Stopping briefly to slam the door behind him, he carried the bike down the stairs, the crazy rebounding echoes of his feet on the steps like the pounding of his heart. How long had he been in the flat—maybe twenty minutes, tops? And it was barely six A.M. on a Monday. Surely they— whoever "they" were—couldn't have sent anyone so fast?

The screech of rubber on tarmac gave him his answer as he threw open the outer door. Feeling sick, Adam jumped down the steps and froze as a large car, a burgundy Daimler, slowly rounded the corner.

He stared. *Oh, my God. . . .*

One of the Daimler's rear windows was opening. The next moment, a gun muzzle appeared, and the car started screaming down the street toward him.

13 PURSUIT

Heart bouncing off his ribs, Adam jumped recklessly onto his bike and raced away. Behind him, the growl of the Daimler's engine rose to a roar. He glanced back.

There was good old Frankie Bateman, in the front passenger seat. Josephs's head of security, back on his tail.

A bicycle against a V-8, thought Adam, pushing himself harder, faster. *Not much of a contest.* He swung right onto Howe Street. There were no alleyways to duck down, no shelter.

Behind him, he heard the thrum of the Daimler as it pulled out into the road. No rubber-burning antics this time. It accelerated smoothly, deliberately.

As though the driver knew that his prey could not escape.

Adam powered along the street on his bike, the wheels humming over the flat cobbles. Muscles in his calves burned as he pedaled. The wind wolfed at his ears. He kept heading north, a single, desperate plan solid in his frantic thoughts. He knew he couldn't outrun the car, but if he could just turn left up ahead. . . .

Luck was with him—if you could call it that. As he leaned into the sharp turn, a van was filling the road, heading straight toward him. Its high-pitched horn blared at him and the driver made obscene gestures. *Yep,* thought Adam, swinging his bike clear of the obstacle, *I know I'm going the wrong way up a one-way street, thanks very much.* But the driver of the Daimler was forced to screech to a halt as it tried to take the corner and found the van blocking its path. The horn sounded a second, longer time. Adam glanced back over his shoulder; he saw the Daimler trying to reverse out of the way while the van driver yelled more abuse through his window.

Adam cycled onward, his little victory lending him new strength, careening to the end of the street and the posh private gardens he saw there. He braked, jumped off and, with a mad rush of adrenaline, threw his bike over the railings and into the dense bushes. Then he scrambled over himself, using his sports bag to blunt the black arrowheads that dug into his ribs, and dived into the shrubbery. Dry mouthed and gasping for breath, he pulled off his gray shirt and changed it for a red top. The hat ought to help disguise him too.

He waited in the bushes, watching out for burgundy Daimlers. The mere clamor of the early weekday traffic was starting to build and he decided to stay put for a while. It would be trickier for Bateman to give chase if he spied him in the Monday morning rush hour.

Finally he emerged from the greenery, looking very different now as he lowered his bike over the locked gates of the private gardens and hauled himself after it. He cycled along India Street, looking all about for signs of trouble.

It was going to be a long old ride back to Granton.

○   ○   ○

Adam made it back across the suburbs of North Edinburgh without spotting the Daimler, and no one appeared to be following him, not even mysterious shadows in the sky.

The thought of returning to the dark warehouse and the deadly creature that hid there made his bones cold. But what choice did he have? For a start, the files he needed to show Hayden were in the rucksack. Somehow, he had to persuade Zed to let him out on his own again—with the top secret notes—back across the city to the scientific sprawl of the BioQuarter.

Is that all, he thought.

He cycled onward, the road starting to get busier now with grimy trucks and pickups. But no traffic ventured up the turning that led to the old warehouse. Adam slowed down, enjoying the malty smell blowing over from the breweries, the feel of the strengthening sun on his skin.

But then he saw a huge pile of mud and broken concrete in the wasteland beyond the warehouse. It looked like a dirty great bomb had gone off there.

"Zed?" Full of foreboding, Adam quickened his stroke on the pedals. The metal roll-up at the delivery entrance was fully closed. He bombed up to the fire doors at the side of the building instead, jumped off the bike, took a deep breath and pushed open the doors.

He wasn't expecting the glare. Harsh and yellow, it shone from fluorescent strip lights in the ceiling, the bulbs wrapped in thick scarves of cobweb. There was a hole in here too, concrete and mud piled up high around it. And there was Zed, sitting up in a curiously human posture beside a tangled spaghetti junction of black leads snaking down into the hole.

"What happened here?" Adam stared at him incredulously. "I left you sleeping a few hours ago—when I come back, you've got the electrics working!"

Zed's lethal jaws stretched open in a wide yawn, and he shrugged as if to say, "And your point is . . . ?"

"Did you tap into the power supply from the gas place next door? How would you know how to do that?" Adam marveled at the thick knot of cables. "It's like the bomb disposal stuff again, or the way you flew us halfway around the world to reach Edinburgh right on course. You can do all these incredible things, but still Josephs goes and orders you killed. Why?" He licked his lips. "What did you do?"

Zed scrambled up a little shakily and stalked closer. Adam held himself very still, hoping desperately he hadn't gone too far. The dinosaur creature reached out one muscular, concrete-dusted claw toward him. . . .

And snatched away his sports bag.

"Hey!" Adam protested halfheartedly. "That's just some stuff I packed. In a bit of a rush." The events of the morning piled back suddenly. "I . . . I was chased by Bateman and some other guys out there. They'd rigged a transmitter in my room and I set it off when I broke in. I dunno if it was meant for me, or my dad if he ever escaped. But now Bateman knows I'm here."

Zed stared at him coldly, seeming scarier than ever in the stark shadows thrown by the lights.

"I got away though," Adam quickly continued. "Hid out for a bit, changed my clothes. Lost them."

Suddenly, Zed thrust his face forward, massive teeth bared, and growled a single syllable: "Trick?"

"No!" Adam protested, shaking his head. "They didn't see me come here, I'm sure of it."

Zed clawed open the sports bag and emptied out the contents. The piggy bank cracked open on the damp concrete, bleeding copper change over the damp floor. Adam didn't dare protest as dexterous claws sorted through his belongings—and then closed on the framed photograph of Mr. Adlar and Adam.

The dinosaur beast lifted it slowly, staring at it intently. Then without warning, he opened his gigantic jaws and shoved the picture inside.

"Wait!" Adam shouted, reaching on instinct for the photo.

Zed roared in his face. Adam recoiled, stumbled over and pushed himself away with his feet, terrified. The huge reptile stared down at him, face twisted in a savage snarl.

"Why did you have to do that?" Adam whispered.

"Get. Dad," Zed growled slowly, as if tasting the words and liking them.

"Yeah, well, you *can't* get my dad, can you?" Adam muttered. "You can't find him, or any of the others, not when they're wearing that spray stuff." He raised his voice recklessly, too angry and frightened to much care about the outcome. "Right now, for all your tricks and growls, you're useless, aren't you?"

The creature raised himself to his full, horrifying height and bellowed in anger. He stamped a great scaly foot and the floor jumped and cracked beneath Adam.

"Shout about it all you like!" Adam yelled back. "But

think for a second—Bateman saw me today. That means he'll be looking for me. He might try and catch me again, not realizing you're here too—you could follow my trail back to their hideout and surprise them or something. . . ."

Zed glared down at him, panting hard, his claws flexing.

Cautiously, feeling sick and light-headed, Adam crawled over to his scattered things and picked up his phone. There'd be hardly any juice in it, of course, after five minutes' charging, and if someone *was* able to track his mobile here. . . .

Right now, he had to take that chance.

The screen glowed into life. Adam called up Dad's last text and held it up to Zed. "Can you read? Do you understand?" he said shakily. "It's like I said, whatever he did to you, they *made* him do it."

Zed stared down at the phone.

"Let me take those notes you have to this friend of Dad's," Adam urged him. "He can explain them to me, like you wanted Sedona to do."

"No . . . ," Zed growled. "*Notes*. Y . . . Z. . . ."

Adam frowned. He thought Zed had been listing the last letters of the alphabet because of his name. But what if he was talking about some kind of alphabetical order? "Um . . . I'm sorry, the papers got mixed up," he said. "All the more reason we show them to someone who really understands them, right? Jeff Hayden is a scientist, and Dad must have chosen him for a reason. He might even know how to find Josephs. We both want that, right?"

"NO!" Zed stamped his foot again, cracking the moldering concrete. "*Zed* find."

"How?" Adam demanded. "What'll you do, fly around the city till you get lucky?"

Zed pushed his face toward Adam's and bared his deadly teeth. "Stay," he hissed.

Adam nodded dumbly, cowed into submission. *To him,* I'm *the animal,* he realized.

Then Zed turned, his wings unfolding from the crevice in his back. He whacked a red button in the wall with his tail and the roll-up door started clanking open.

"If you're seen, you'll start a panic!" Adam warned him. "There'll be police, army, riot squads coming after you. You won't be able to stop them all. You'll die, and this time you won't come back!"

But the huge animal ignored Adam, launching himself into the air.

Adam ran over to the doorway, watched Zed fade from view to become little more than a blur against the sky's pale blue. "And I hope you *do* die," he yelled after him, "you scaly son of a . . ."

He can probably still hear you.

Adam turned away and kicked the wall in frustration. "Ow!" he shouted, crossly. He slammed his palm against the red button on the wall and the door clanked down to shut out the sky.

His phone chimed suddenly.

Adam stared down, his heart flipping. Three messages, left queuing all this time, had finally found their way through. Nothing from Dad. Just the usual stuff from his mates—a forwarded joke, and some good-natured abuse for not bothering to keep in touch. He touched the little words on the screen with his fingers.

Josephs could be tracking me through this, he thought. *Right now.*

As Adam turned off the phone, he had never felt lonelier. Here he was, in a crumbling, damp ruin, with men out to get him, monsters ready to kill him, Dad out of reach—and him an escaped fugitive with not a clue what to do about any of it.

He sat down on a square of old carpet and put his head in his hands.

o o o

Adam woke with a start. The door was clanking open. He got unsteadily to his feet and hid behind one of the giant rolls of carpet, checking his watch. It was past seven in the evening. He'd slept the whole day away.

It was Zed who came thumping inside, alone, and Adam didn't know whether to feel relieved or afraid.

The giant's eyes looked darker and meaner than ever as he hit the door button and the metal segments clanked back down behind him. He stood quivering for a few moments. Then, with a deafening roar he smashed his tail against the wall. As the impact boomed out and damp concrete jumped from the wall in showers, Zed stamped over to the rolls of carpet and hurled himself down on top of them, his breath coming quickly in short rasps. Adam backed away, transfixed as Zed turned first one side of his face to the rotten fabric, then the other.

That's what I do, he realized. He could picture himself after a typical row with Dad, chucking himself on the bed and pressing his hot face against the cool pillow, trying to calm down. . . .

"It's one thing to take my moves from Ultra-Reality," Adam whispered. "But this is me you're ripping off. The real me."

The creature did not respond. Adam raised his voice. "You didn't find Josephs or Dad or anyone out there . . . did you?"

Zed looked over at Adam as if noticing him for the first time. Then, slowly, he shook his head. Adam saw that there was wetness in the animal's sharp, black eyes.

"Maybe"—Adam swallowed hard—"maybe we could try it my way, then. Tomorrow?"

The dinosaur turned away, hunched over on his side.

Adam nodded and walked slowly, quietly away, giving the beast his space. He understood. He'd lost enough arguments himself in the past. In time, Zed would come around.

"How about that." He looked over at the dinosaur's vast, alien bulk and shivered. "I know just how you feel."

14 CONTACT

It was past three in the morning, and Adam couldn't sleep. The lights were out now in case anyone came looking, but the power cables were still humming loudly, a sound like giant flies circling in the darkness. The noise, anxious thoughts about his dad and fears that a burgundy Daimler might be pulling up just outside were all keeping Adam horribly alert.

Zed's snoring wasn't helping matters. The creature had said and done little more after his giant sulk, falling into a deep slumber, his head crushing the collapsing rolls of carpet. Somehow, Zed's heavy silence was almost as unnerving as his full-on rage.

Hoping for distraction, Adam turned on his dad's phone. There was a little power left in the battery, even after all these weeks, and the glow of the screen was like a tiny night-light in the cold, dark warehouse. As the wind blew haunting notes through the broken panes, he started browsing the files.

There were loads of really boring work emails that went way over his head. He skimmed over most of them. One was from Jeff Hayden, sent a few months back, asking how Dad was doing and mentioning he'd won this amazing amount of funding for his company. Addresses for both work and home were stored in his profile, much to Adam's relief.

Then he saw an email sent from Sam Josephs.

Adam sat bolt upright, staring at the phone. "So you already knew him," he murmured, opening the file. It was dated over a year ago.

Josephs was ranting at Dad for firing him from the Ultra-Reality gaming project. He'd wanted to take the research in other "more valuable" directions.

"Repetitive, manual labor could be taken over by animals instead of robots for a fraction of the cost," Adam read aloud under his breath. "Stray dogs could be turned into perfect helpmates for the disabled overnight. Primates could be instructed to perform complex tasks in high-risk environments in minutes. . . ."

He looked across at Zed. *Or dinosaurs could be trained to hack into power supplies and defuse bombs.*

Made into modern-day killing machines.

"But how do you get your hands on a living dinosaur?" he whispered into the darkness. "And why would you want to?"

The grunts and growls of Zed in his troubled sleep were Adam's only answer.

o o o

Zed was sullen later that morning. He didn't respond to Adam's nervous attempts at conversation, apparently absorbed by the MP3 player he'd found in the sports bag. It looked tiny in his huge hand, but using the tips of his claws he had got it working. A Kings of Leon track was ringing tinnily from the in-ear headphones. The dinosaur sniffed the little device suspiciously.

"It's just a music player," Adam said. "Dad used to plug it into the car stereo on journeys. A lot of the songs on there are his old rubbish, but he let me stick on a few albums. . . ."

Zed growled as if telling him to be quiet. The beat went on spilling from the headphones.

"I was going to take it with me on the bus," Adam said boldly. "I'm going to the BioQuarter."

"Adam, back," he grumbled. "Two hours."

"That's not long enough," Adam protested. "People like Mr. Hayden, they have appointments and stuff. I don't know when he'll be able to see me."

Zed snorted and jabbed a claw at a button. The song changed to one of Dad's—"Ruby Tuesday" by the Rolling Stones.

"That one's almost as old as you are," muttered Adam. He took a deep breath. "Look, Zed, I need more time. I was thinking at least—"

"Four," the dinosaur rasped.

"Yeah, four hours. Two o'clock," Adam agreed, slightly taken aback. "I'll know if he can see me by then. If not, maybe I can try tomorrow." *Any excuse to get away from you,* he thought. "I've got enough cash for the bus fare. And after yesterday, Josephs will be looking for a boy on a bike, won't he?"

"Jo . . . sephs," Zed snarled, grinding his enormous teeth.

At least it's not Dad's name he's chewing up, thought Adam, remembering the picture frame that vanished into Zed's jaws yesterday. "Josephs used to work with my dad, but he got fired. That's why he must be out to get him." Adam paused. "You believe me about Dad now, right?"

Zed let out a long, hissing breath. Was it just the weird light through the mucky windows, or did he look paler than before?

"I'll see you soon," Adam said awkwardly.

The brooding beast made no reply. Mick Jagger's voice leaked from the headphones, singing about losing your dreams and losing your mind.

o o o

The BioQuarter in Little France was a new development on the outskirts of the city, bringing together loads of different "life science" companies and education sites. In addition to Edinburgh's main hospital, there were outposts of the university, the Queen's Medical Research Institute and a giant hundred-acre biomedical research park filled with hundreds of high-tech businesses, all at the cutting edge of genetic exploration.

As the bus trundled southward, Adam remembered his dad going on about how Dolly, the world's first cloned sheep, was created here in Edinburgh. Basically, scientists took a cell from one sheep and used it to grow another sheep that was exactly the same—like a living photocopy.

Zed was no simple photocopy of anything that had ever lived, of that Adam was sure. Not with his sharp mind and his dragon wings. His cells would have to be something special. Was that a clue as to why Dad had directed Adam to this gleaming new development of steel and glass, where science and sci-fi clashed in billion-dollar surroundings?

Adam wandered about, his sports bag heavy with files, ignoring the curious glances he attracted, until he found the device and diagnostic companies cluster.

And there, at last, were the ultramodern offices of Symtek Biotronics.

He walked into a spotless reception area. The futuristic chairs looked as uncomfortable as he felt approaching the slender young woman behind the desk—who might have been cloned from a Barbie doll. Adam saw Jeff Hayden's name on the wall, listed as Symtek's director of scientific development.

"I need to see Mr. Hayden, please," he told her. "I'm Adam Adlar, Bill Adlar's son."

The name clearly meant nothing to her. "Mr. Hayden is busy." Glossy pink lips pouted doubtfully. "Do you have an appointment?"

"No. But it's important. Is he in today?"

"He really is *very* busy."

Adam leaned forward over her desk. "Um, I know I'm not your typical visitor here, but this is important. Honestly, the most important thing ever. . . ." He gave his best shot at a winning smile. "Please?"

He was spared Barbie's response because just then the door behind him opened and an imposing, portly man in a crumpled blue suit and a floppy red bow tie strode in. He was tanned, maybe in his early fifties, with combed-over hair standing up like it was partying on his bald, shiny head. His shoes were muddy and his briefcase was scuffed, but his green eyes twinkled with humor.

"Sorry I'm late, Megan, my meeting overran," said the man, a transatlantic twang to his deep voice. He noticed Adam and looked taken aback for a moment. "Don't tell me this is my eleven o'clock appointment?"

"Young Mr. Adlar arrived unexpectedly," said Megan, wearing her best Barbie smile. "He's just leaving."

Adam ignored her. "Mr. Hayden?" he asked breathlessly.

The man nodded, his frown deepening. "Adlar? Then, you're Bill's son?"

"Yes—Adam!" He could've dissolved into a puddle of sheer relief. "I've come all the way from America to see you."

"Oh?" Hayden smiled politely. "That's quite a trip, Adam. Your dad keeping well? I haven't seen him in an age. Didn't he go out to New Mexico?"

"Aye, he went out there."

"Well, you must tell him to pop by sometime," said Hayden. "I'm a little preoccupied right now, but—"

"Please, Mr. Hayden, this is really urgent." Adam clutched the sports bag to his chest. "Could we talk in your office? Since you've got twenty minutes before your next appointment, and all. . . ."

Hayden hesitated. Then his face softened as he shrugged and smiled. "I guess it wouldn't kill me to take five. Let's go."

With a smile at Megan and some silent thanks to the gods of good timing, Adam followed Hayden eagerly into a spacious office. One wall was lined with bookcases, crammed with volumes on everything from advanced biology to theories of evolution and . . .

"Dinosaurs," Adam blurted out loud, crossing to take a closer look at an oversized book. He noticed the name HAYDEN was printed on the spine. "Wow, did you write this?"

"Years ago. That one and a few others," said Hayden, smiling. "They're a little dated now. But I've always had something of a passion for prehistory. Spent holidays and gap years researching theories, digging around for fossils in all weathers. . . . Your father used to say I was crazy." He chuckled fondly. "I've been meaning to catch up with him properly, especially now that Symtek's relocated to Edinburgh."

Adam smiled and nodded. He was dying to just blurt out his reasons for being here; here was a grown-up, someone who really knew about dinosaurs, who could help. But he didn't want Hayden to think he was just some silly, panicking kid. "You, er . . . you like it here in Scotland?"

"What's not to like? Once you get used to the weather!" He settled himself into a comfy leather chair behind a battered old oak desk. A wafer-thin iMac computer stood incongruously on top of it. "I live out in St. Leonards, close to Arthur's Seat. Beautiful country. Oh, but I'm forgetting my manners. . . ." He opened a desk drawer, pulled out a crumpled clear plastic bag and offered it to Adam with an encouraging smile. "Organic gingersnap? All local ingredients."

Adam took one politely, wondering how he could get to the point without sounding like a maniac.

"You know, you remind me of your dad in his younger days," said Hayden, crunching on a cookie with enthusiasm. "We met at Stanford. Both of us doing our doctorates at the School of Engineering." Hayden leaned back in his chair and grinned. "It's a good thing he came straight to Edinburgh afterward—I'd never have handled the competition! Your dad's a brilliant man, Adam. Of course, our careers have taken us in very different directions now; him with his gaming, me moving into biomedicine. . . ."

"You mean, pills and stuff?" Adam hazarded.

"More like solving problems in clinical medicine through study of how the body works." Hayden licked crumbs from his lips and leaned forward again. "It's very exciting at the moment. We're developing what we call an accelerated bioregenerator."

Adam blinked. "A what-was-that?"

"Bioregenerator. It's not so complicated!" Hayden assured him. "Think of living creatures. Our bodies are programmed to self-repair, given the chance, right? Cuts scab over, bones rejoin and heal if they're set correctly. A lizard can even grow itself a new tail." His eyes glittered with excitement. "Now, imagine if we could *accelerate* the healing process—repair damaged tissue faster and more efficiently. People with life-threatening injuries could make a full recovery in hours rather than days or weeks."

Adam thought back to the men Zed had killed back at Fort Ponil. How quickly their lives had been snuffed out. "Sounds amazing," he said.

"I'm sorry." Hayden must have noticed that Adam looked distracted. "You told me something's urgent, and here I am giving you the sponsorship spiel. What's up?"

"Uh . . ." Adam decided to jump in headfirst. "Dad went missing in New Mexico."

Hayden frowned. "Missing?"

"About three weeks ago, he said he had to go and work at a different lab—and he never came home." Adam could feel tears welling up and resolutely swallowed them back. "But he did get one text through to me, telling me to go and see you with evidence of a secret project he'd been made to work on. The Z. rex project."

"Z. rex? As in T. rex?" said Hayden doubtfully. "Look, Adam, if this is some sort of joke—"

"I'm not joking."

"Well, then, the police would surely—"

"Dad said I shouldn't tell the police. Said they couldn't help."

"Then who *have* you told?"

Adam hesitated. *What do I say—that the only one who knows is the talking dinosaur who flew me across the Atlantic on his back?* "Uh, no one," he said at last, deciding it was best to let out the details a few at a time. "I've been on my own. Managed to get back home, but . . . anyway, Dad said that you could show the evidence to the right people."

"What evidence? What people?" Hayden looked baffled. "And what does 'Z. rex' even mean?"

"The *Z* stands for 'zenith,'" Adam said, reaching into his sports bag for the files. "This is a whole new kind of dinosaur."

"A new fossil, you mean?" The scientist scratched his head and sent his hair madly dancing. "What does any of this have to do with Bill going missing?"

"Just about everything." Adam solemnly piled the files on the desk. "I . . . I managed to get hold of these. Reports on the Z. rex project. I don't really understand them, but if you're a scientist and know all about dinosaurs, then maybe . . ."

Hayden flipped open the first of the files. "Re-engineering a dinosaur," he muttered, his fingers flicking through the crumpled, dog-eared pages. "Force-evolving cells? Rejuvenation of fossil matter?" He looked up, eyebrows riding the frames of his glasses. "Adam, I say again, if this is some kind of joke—"

"It's no joke, I promise. Have you heard of a company called Geneflow Solutions? Or someone called Sam Josephs?"

"I've heard of her." Hayden's face had hardened a little. "Why?"

"Her?" Adam echoed, surprised.

Hayden nodded. "Sam's a she. *Samantha* Josephs."

"Well . . . if it's the same person, *she* is running the Z. rex project. She used to work for Dad, but Dad fired her."

"I gave her a job myself," said Hayden, "some time ago. Brilliant girl, expert in animal neurology—that's study of the nervous system. She oversaw early trials of my bioregenerators on injured animals." He took off his glasses and stared into space. "Turned out to be a corporate spy, selling the information to the highest bidder."

Adam sat up straighter in his chair. "Maybe she was doing the same on Dad's Ultra-Reality project?"

"Perhaps," said Hayden cautiously.

"Well, in any case, she's forcing Dad to work for her." Adam scowled. "He went to work at this place called Fort Ponil and never came back. She was holding him there."

"Kidnapping? I can't imagine she would stoop to that." Hayden bit into another cookie and looked again at the files. "Then again, I couldn't imagine anyone taking cell research as far as this. The experimentation involved, the sheer cost . . ." He turned another page, reacted to the information printed there and shook his head. "Your father knows, of course, that I'm a private sector adviser to the International Science and Ethics Association."

"The what?"

"Whenever new breakthroughs in genetic experiments are made, the United Nations calls on me and various others to consider the ethics involved and rule on whether the work should be allowed to continue." He looked troubled. "Maybe that's another reason why Bill sent you to see me. If someone has taken these theories and applied them to a living animal . . ."

"Mr. Hayden, what can we do?" Adam asked plaintively. "Geneflow Solutions has a base somewhere in Edinburgh. Josephs and my dad could both be there."

"I can't believe that Josephs would have the nerve to show her face around here again." Hayden finished his gingersnap and looked at Adam. "You know, I really think you should tell the police what you've told me."

"Dad told me not to. No way, he said."

"But you've heard nothing from him since that text message?"

"No," Adam admitted. "But if I do tell the police, and Josephs finds out, she might"—he bit his lip— "might hurt him, or . . ."

Hayden sighed and waved a hand, as if dismissing the idea. "Okay. I agree we don't tell them right now. Let me read through these files. I'll do some discreet asking around the local science community, see if I can turn up anything on Geneflow Solutions. And I'll even ask my contacts at the UN if anyone's approached them regarding this Z. rex project."

"You will?" Adam's shoulders felt suddenly way lighter. "That would be awesome, thank you."

He passed Adam a business card. "If you think of anything else that might help, just call me. Anytime. Where are you staying, by the way?"

"Uh . . . with a friend." *Not a giant dinosaur in the shell of a warehouse over at Granton, oh, no.* "I'm using Dad's old phone, you can get me on that. . . ."

He scribbled the number on the top page of the nearest open file.

"Thanks." Hayden surveyed the files again, shaking his head. "I'll ring if I hear something."

"If," Adam echoed glumly.

"Let's regenerate that 'if' into a 'when,' shall we?" Hayden smiled confidently. "Try not to worry. We'll get to the bottom of this, because I hate mysteries. That's why I went into research for a living!"

Adam smiled back. For a few moments in that sunlit office, things seemed okay and the right way round again—the adult stepping in to sort stuff out. He carried some of that optimism with him as he headed back across the sci-fi landscape of the research park.

It was only once he'd returned to the rougher reality of the city that the fear and the nerves ebbed back. For all Hayden's words and Adam's hopes, his dad was still out there. And still lost.

15 SLAUGHTER

Adam stopped off at a tourist restaurant on his way back. His stomach had been growling, and he suddenly realized there was nothing he wanted more than hot, fleshy French fries, half buried under small mountains of salt and then smothered in ketchup. He ate slowly at a table while discreetly charging his dad's phone from a socket in the wall, and kept a watchful eye for passing friends and burgundy Daimlers. In the end he barely tasted a thing.

He was wondering now if he *should* have told Hayden about Z. rex being here. *Maybe I should have invited him to the warehouse to meet Zed for himself. What's that old saying? "Seeing is believing."*

Or—more likely in this case—*"Seeing is running away*

screaming calling the army to come and blow up the giant dinosaur."

"You did the right thing," he told himself. "For now, at least."

He bought a couple of energy drinks and left the café through the little window in the men's room. Just in case he was being watched.

o o o

It was close to one-fifteen by the time Adam got off the bus in Leith and started walking back toward the warehouse. He wondered how much he should tell Zed, shivering at the thought of going back into the clammy darkness of the monster's lair. He wanted to hold on to the sunlight just a little longer. He wanted Mr. Hayden to ring him right away, with good news.

At least I've told someone, he reflected, pausing beside a large, muddy field. *It's out now.*

There were five horses in the field. Three of them were lying down, legs folded, while two others cropped the short grass.

Then one of the feeding horses, large and gray, looked up at the trees on the outskirts of the field and snorted nervously. The horse beside it lifted its head. A shiver of unease seemed to run through the group. Those lying down got to their feet, ears moving nervously backward and forward, eyes wary and nostrils wide. Something had them spooked.

Adam watched, curious, as the first horse started to circle the group at a trot, his tail high. The younger horses in the middle jostled together anxiously.

Then, Adam felt his insides lurch as a blur of green scales suddenly appeared, bounding out of the trees. The horses scattered, ears back, muscles bunching and stretching as they galloped away.

"Zed, no!" Adam yelled, but the words were lost beneath the pounding of hooves. "Don't!"

The horses couldn't escape. The wood and wire fence was there, hemming them in. Zed burst into flight, overtook the large, gray horse that had scented him first and landed directly in front of it. It swerved aside but too late to avoid a tail swipe that knocked it to the ground with a sickening crunch. Eyes wide and terrified, it tried to rise but the huge, crushing teeth were already sinking into its sides. Adam turned away, nauseated, and the smallest horse caught his attention. It was cantering in frantic circles, whinnying in distress. Zed flapped briefly into the air like some terrible dragon and landed right on top of it, stamping its hindquarters into the muddy earth.

As Zed began to feed, Adam crouched down behind a fencepost and tried to hold on to his lunch.

This was not the sharply skilled bird-killer he'd seen on the beach in Ontario, or the cunning shark fisher. As the remaining horses dodged and shied in blind panic, Zed turned from the bloody remains of his meal to goad them—hopping about, roaring and clawing at whichever came closest. There seemed no strategy at work. He was playing with his food.

Finally Zed landed a heavy blow to another of the horses. It collapsed to the ground, bloody stripes marking its neck. The dinosaur roared in triumph, bore down over it, jaws widening. As he did so, just for a moment, his eyes met Adam's.

Adam recoiled. There was no recognition in the beast's gaze. Only crazed hunger.

Then suddenly the monster shut his eyes, shook his head like something sharp was stuck inside it. The remaining horses cowered back as Zed's vast bulk seemed to shimmer and all but vanish, before the dinosaur left his kill and launched himself up into the sky and away from the carnage.

Adam stared after the dragon shadow on the air, feeling sick to his stomach. *He didn't even seem to know who I was.*

If he hadn't taken off when he did . . . would he have attacked me as well?

The rising note of an engine roused Adam as a car drove past. Lucky for the driver he hadn't chanced by just two minutes earlier.

Adam walked unsteadily onward. Visions of the hunt pooled in his thoughts, vivid as the bloodstains slowly baking into the mud and grass.

o o o

It was well past two o'clock by the time Adam neared the warehouse. He had lingered as long as he dared, in no hurry to face the dinosaur again. Obviously Zed had to eat meat, but it was the pleasure he seemed to take in the slaughter that gave Adam the chills. When would Zed next need to feed?

Reluctantly, Adam quickened his step as he turned up the quiet lane that led to the warehouse yard.

"I'm here," he called warily as he approached the fire doors. He didn't want to go inside. "Are you back?"

There was no reply beyond the angry hum of the lashed-up cables and a slow, ragged panting. That answered his question.

Steeling himself, Adam went in—and frowned. The lights were on, showing Zed sprawled awkwardly over his bed of dank carpet. He seemed pale again and he was shivering. In the space of half an hour, he'd gone from lethal attacker to feeble animal; the difference couldn't have been greater. The MP3 player was on the floor, the ghostly echoes of music still sounding from the headphones, slurring slightly as the batteries wore down.

For a few seconds, Adam hung back by the door and regarded him, warily silent. The wild, hideous strength he'd seen Zed use in the field seemed to have fled the dinosaur's body, but he was taking no chances.

"You're not looking so good," Adam said at last, a hard edge to his voice. "Maybe something you ate disagreed with you?"

"Ad," Zed croaked. "Am . . . Ad . . . am."

Adam frowned. Zed had never called him by his name before. He moved cautiously closer. "You grabbed your head out there when you . . . Well. Is it your head hurting?"

The black eyes gazed at him, unfocused. "Pain. Brain."

Adam chewed on a fingernail. This wasn't the confrontation he'd been expecting. Feeling an unexpected tug of sympathy, he came closer still and stooped to switch off the MP3 player.

Zed thumped the tip of his tail suddenly, growling like a guard dog. Adam left the player alone and quickly straightened up again. "I don't know what to do," he said. "It's not like I can call a vet."

"Jo . . . sephs." Zed struggled weakly to rise, but couldn't do it. "Jo . . . sephs. Pain. Dark."

Maybe he had some kind of fit, thought Adam. *That's why he went crazy out there.* "I wish I knew what you were really trying to tell me," he said. "I found out stuff about Josephs. She's a woman for one thing— could you not have told me that?"

"Pain, dark," Zed repeated. He closed his eyes, pursed his scaly lips carefully. "Past . . . pictures. Dark."

"Past pictures?" Adam had a flash of inspiration. "You mean, memories? You can't remember stuff?"

"Get." The dinosaur strained again to lift his head. "File. Man read?"

"Uh . . . he's started to, yeah." Adam shifted uncomfortably. "He's going to help us find Josephs.

"Files," Zed snarled. "Files tell Adam. Y, Z."

Adam frowned. "Uh, I did tell you the order got all messed up. But I'm sure he'll read through them all."

"FILES!" roared the dinosaur. Struggling up angrily, he towered over Adam. "Y . . . Z!"

"I'm sorry!" Adam cowered away. "I didn't know you wanted the last files straight back, I . . ." He trailed off, his thoughts racing around a sudden possibility. Wait a second. . . . *Y, Z.*

You mean, Why Z—why Zed?

"You don't know any more than I do about where you came from . . . do you?"

Zed stared down at him, panting hard.

"Is that why you wanted Sedona to read the files at Fort Ponil out loud—to 'tell Zed'? Is that why you bothered to keep him alive?"

The dinosaur sat back down heavily, shaking the entire warehouse. "Am Ad. Why Zed."

"Am Ad . . . ?" Adam felt the concrete seem to lurch beneath him, and wiped a sweaty hand through his hair. "Oh, boy. When your brain was hurt, maybe those bits of my brain waves you picked up from Ultra got tangled with your own. . . ."

Making you more dangerous and unpredictable than ever.

Oh, Dad, what did you do?

"Jo . . . sephs," Zed said again, hoarsely. "Dark."

"I can shed a bit of light on her," Adam murmured. "Mr. Hayden said she's some sort of corporate spy. She steals, like, technology secrets and sells them to whoever pays the most."

Zed closed his eyes and took a deep, shuddering breath.

"Thing is, was she trying to sell you, or did she steal other secrets to make you?" Adam pondered. "'Force-evolving cells,' that was one of the things Mr. Hayden said. And 'rejuvenation of fossil matter'—I think that means making it younger. Ring any bells with you?"

The question was answered with a wet snort.

"Thinking about it, though . . ." Adam chewed a fingernail, musing aloud. "What if she stole secrets from my dad last year? From the Ultra-Reality system, I mean. And she's been working on her own version, but something happened that meant she needed *Dad* as well as his Think-Send tech. . . ." He felt a speck of excitement start to snowball. "And it was her, or Bateman, who robbed Dad's employers in New Mexico to get the U-R equipment—which had my fight moves stored in the memory! Don't you get it, Zed? That would mean Dad really *isn't* the one to blame for what happened to you."

Zed didn't answer for a while. When he did, his voice was husky and faint. "Dad . . . hurt. Why Zed?"

"I don't know," Adam murmured, the brief rush of elation draining away. There were so many questions, so many ifs and maybes—and Zed, the focus of them all, lying there like a fallen giant, unable to give any answers because they'd been burned from his brain. "I'm sorry."

What if Zed died?

Wouldn't that be best? thought Adam, with a twinge of guilt. No more risk of him tearing into the people of the city. Or tearing into Dad, if he ever found him. He didn't belong in this world. It was like Bateman had said—Zed was a freak.

But for all that, Adam still felt conflicted. This was a real, live genetically modified dinosaur for heaven's sake, capable of the most incredible things. Including murder and destruction. . . . What he'd seen today with those horses was only the tip of the iceberg.

He glanced toward the fire doors. *Perhaps I could try going outside?* He chewed his lip. *Perhaps I could run. I could find Mr. Hayden again; now that he's got the files, I can tell him what really happened.*

"Ad not go," Zed ground out suddenly, as if listening in on his thoughts. "Stay."

Adam closed his eyes. "It's all right, Zed. I'm not going anywhere."

He sat down and listened to the whine of power resonating through his concrete prison, and the tinny drone from the headphones. Sat there, waiting for another day to end.

16 FALTER

Dad's phone went off in Adam's pocket. He woke with a start, fumbling for the handset, blinking away the sleep. His watch showed it was past eleven o'clock, and the lights were still burning in the warehouse; Zed didn't seem to have stirred, his breathing still ragged and labored. *What if someone's seen we're here?* Adam thought frantically.

Then he saw the words on Dad's screen: JEFF MOBILE. He felt a jolt of anticipation and accepted the call. "This is Adam, hello?"

"Adam, hey, it's Jeff Hayden. I'm sorry to call you so late."

"It's fine," Adam said quickly. "I'm up. Um, everyone's up. Have you heard anything about Dad?"

"I'm making progress." There was a pause. "Adam, those files you gave me . . . are there any more of them?"

"No . . ." He glanced over at Zed. "That was all I could take with me."

"It's incredible, Adam." Hayden's voice sounded strained. "If these notes are genuine, then I believe these people have managed to re-create a living, breathing dinosaur. What's more, they used stolen Symtek bioregenerator technology to help them achieve it."

"They . . . they did?" Adam swallowed hard. *Zed had healed so quickly after the shark savaged his arm, and he'd survived the brain-blast—it made sense that he'd been exposed to something that helped his body fix itself faster.* "That's uh . . . wow. So, have you found out where Josephs might be?"

"I've got nothing on Geneflow Solutions so far, but I managed to track down an address for Josephs herself, off the Royal Mile. This could be the biggest breakthrough in modern science since we split the atom. It could literally change the world—but if they stole Symtek's technology to make it happen. . . ."

"They could've taken Dad's too," said Adam.

"Intellectual property theft is Josephs's specialty," Hayden agreed. "She must have been helping herself to all sorts of cutting-edge technology." He paused, as if marshaling his thoughts. "My first instinct was to go straight to the police—"

"My dad said not to."

"I know. And in any case, if it gets out that blue-prints for our bioregenerators have been given to another company . . ." Hayden whistled. "Believe me, Symtek can do without that kind of publicity. Our stock value would plummet."

Adam glanced over at Zed, whose eyelids were twitch-ing, and lowered his voice. "So what *are* you going to do?"

"I'm going to call on Josephs tomorrow morning and insist that she speak with me at Symtek with lawyers present," Hayden declared. "I'll confront her with the evidence you've given me—and I think perhaps you should be there too."

"Right." Adam's insides twitched at the thought of coming face to face with the woman who had turned his world into wreckage. "Of course. I'll be there."

"And either she lets your dad go free, or else I'll *have* to go to the police with what we know."

"But . . . what if she tries to stop us? She's got these men working for her, security types." Adam thought of bruised-faced Bateman and shuddered. "They tried to catch me in New Mexico."

"They *what*?" Hayden paused. "Why didn't you say so before? Look, Adam, I can only really help if you come completely clean with me."

"I *have* come clean with you." As he spoke, Zed shifted noisily onto his side and let out a colossal fart. It sounded like a small explosion.

"Say again?"

"Sorry, it's a bad line," Adam said quickly, running for the fire doors. "All that really happened is that some men came to Dad's apartment. Proper hard men. They tried to get me to go with them someplace. But I managed to get away from them. . . ." *With a little help.* "Went straight to the airport and came here."

There was a long pause. Adam tried not to choke on the smell of Zed's horrific wind, strong enough to strip the lining from his lungs.

"Sounds like you've been through an awful lot," Hayden said at last. "Well, don't worry. Symtek's got its own security. And I'll make sure that Josephs knows I've given full details from those files of yours to my friends at the UN, including her address. She won't dare lift a finger against us."

And we can get Dad away, Adam thought in a rush of excitement. *We can maybe get Zed back under wraps, looked after by experts—and the baddies all sent down to jail.*

He ached at the thought of seeing Dad again. Could this be it? The beginning of the end of the whole ordeal?

"Adam?" Hayden prompted.

"Sorry. I'm fine. I'm great." He cleared his throat. "So where's this address?"

"Lawnmarket, over in the Old Town," Hayden said. "For safety's sake, how about we meet just around the corner? Bottom of The Mound, say . . . beside the Scott Monument?"

"Right."

"Say about nine?"

"Whenever." Adam eyed the sleeping Zed nervously. "That should be fine."

"Just one thing—I want you to promise you'll stay with my security men and let me do all the talking, right?"

"Yes. Yes, I will."

"This will need very careful handling." Hayden paused again. "You can't imagine what this Z. rex stuff might mean for the world."

Wanna bet? thought Adam, looking over at Zed. He spoke in a small voice. "I just want my dad back, Mr. Hayden."

"We'll get him back, Adam. I promise." Adam could hear the warmth in Hayden's voice, and drew some comfort from it. "I'll meet you tomorrow. Good night— and try to get some sleep."

"Night," Adam said, and killed the connection—just as Zed started to stretch, his jaws swinging open in a low, rasping yawn. The dinosaur noticed the lights were still blazing, got up with only a little difficulty and stomped across to the cables. He yanked them apart, sending sparks dancing. The lights went out and the buzzing changed pitch.

"You seem a bit better," Adam remarked. "Except it smells like something crawled up your butt and died there."

"Drink," came the deep, throaty whisper in the dark. "Hungry. Ad . . . stay."

Like a good wee doggie. Adam sighed as Zed staggered over to the loading bay and clanked open the doors. *Outside's the best place for you. But come tomorrow morning, it'll be my turn to go for a walk. . . .* He heard wings unfolding, the stamp of scaly tiptoes on the concrete. Then the beast lurched away, escaping into the night.

Adam let out a long, shaky breath. "Lock up your horses, Edinburgh," he muttered grimly.

Alone again.

Tomorrow, this could all be over. Adam clung to the thought like a little kid might clutch at a teddy bear for comfort as he lay down on his damp sleeping bag. Too bone-weary to do anything but dream of somewhere safe, far away from here.

o   o   o

The new day began for Adam with the usual chill of the damp concrete bleeding into his bones. Only this time, excitement was seeping through as well. *This is the day something happens,* he thought, willing it to be true. *The day I start getting my life back.*

Zed had come back after an hour or so at large. Adam had held dead still and pretended to be asleep when the creature shambled back in, scraping his tail along the ground.

Around seven-thirty, Adam rose and dressed, crunched on a mint and swigged from a can of flat Coke. He was fizzing himself, with nerves. And he still hadn't asked permission to go out this morning.

He crossed a little closer to where the dinosaur laid resting, sunlight falling on him in squares through the dirty windows. Zed's skin was still mottled with paler patches, and the shadow of dried blood haunted his jaws. Adam noticed lumps of fleece, smeared sticky and black, lying in the shadows. *Must be working his way through the whole farmyard,* he thought darkly.

Adam cleared his throat. "You, uh . . . you any better, then?"

Zed's eyes opened. They seemed blacker than ever.

"I need to go out," Adam announced boldly. "To get those files back from Dad's friend I saw yesterday."

Zed blinked, scaly eyelids chopping down like the blades of twin guillotines. "No. Ad stay."

"I won't be gone long. . . ." Adam cleared his throat. "This man's going to tell me all about you. And help find Dad."

Zed remained silent for long, heavy seconds. "Come back," the creature said at last, carefully arranging its lips around the words.

"Back?" Adam was taken off guard. "Yeah, of course I'll come back. Soon as I can." *Only it might just be with company*, he thought guiltily. "Things . . . they're going to work out, Zed. You'll see."

The scaly eyelids flickered closed, and Zed resumed his silence.

o o o

The Scott Monument, with its soot-blackened spires, pointed bleakly at the clouds like a stone rocket that could never fly. But Adam's hopes were doing their best to zoom into orbit as he cycled through the fumy, traffic-choked bustle of Princes Street. He was half an hour early for his rendezvous, but better that than late. He hurtled past the Royal Scottish Academy with its pillars and banners and make-believe gaslights, past the big stores and the tourist shops with their tartan-towel souvenirs.

He passed the monument—no sign of Hayden as yet—and swung a left onto St. David Street, heading for the bike racks at nearby St. Andrew Square. The glass-roofed café in the square's gardens was already doing a roaring trade. Adam parked his bike, jogged past the rows of cars and across the road to the monument and threw himself down on a bench at the end of Princes Street Gardens to catch his breath.

On the journey over he'd gone through a million possibilities in his head. Sam Josephs—a tall, pale ice queen in his imagination—would try to run as soon as she saw Hayden with his security men, and he would join them in chasing after her. Or Frankie Bateman would answer the door, try to attack Adam, only to be beaten back by the guards. Or Josephs would come out holding a gun to Dad's head, and Adam would have to reason with her. . . .

He glanced up worriedly at the sky. What if Zed got the scent of what was happening here and came sailing out of the sky to smash everything?

"It'll be okay," he breathed. It was five to nine. "It's got to be okay."

He paced around the park, killing time. Surveyed the circular beds of tulips and the grassy slope leading down to trees and train tracks. Looked across to Arthur's Seat, the ancient, blocky volcano where he and Zed had first landed. It seemed forever ago, and yet no time at all. The days and nights had melted into a long, frightening blur. But soon . . .

The time had nudged past nine, and no sign of Hayden. "C'mon, c'mon. . . ."

By nine-thirty, nerves were gnawing at Adam's stomach like rats.

By ten, he was getting angry. *He'll be here,* Adam told himself, checking Dad's mobile for the millionth time. *Nothing's happened to him. He's just been delayed.*

So why hasn't he called?

Princes Street was busy with shoppers and tourists

now. Adam wondered with envy what his friends were up to. *School must start in a few days,* he thought vaguely, and then sighed. Ordinary stuff like that, it all belonged to another life.

He started worrying again about Zed. He hadn't given a time when he'd be back; he hadn't really given much thought to returning to Zed at all. He'd been focusing only on finding his dad again. And after all Dad must have been through, he couldn't imagine he'd be keen on rushing to the waterfront to meet and greet the giant monster he'd half killed; the dinosaur who'd come here for revenge.

At ten-thirty, stomach churning, Adam pulled out Hayden's business card from his jeans pocket and decided to call. The mobile number went straight to voice mail.

"Hello, it's Adam. I'm waiting where we said. Please call when you can. Bye."

He waited another few minutes and tried Symtek's offices. The familiar bored voice of Megan the Barbie receptionist came through loud and clear: "I'm afraid he's out of the office today. Would you like to be put through to his voice mail?"

"No, thanks. Are his, um, security people there?"

"Who is this?"

"Adam Adlar. I was in yesterday. I'm meant to be meeting him right now. Did he leave me any message?"

"No. I don't know about security. You can try him on his mobile."

"I have," Adam mumbled, disconnecting. Perhaps Hayden had tried to call him while he'd been calling the office?

No voice mail message appeared.

When no one had arrived by eleven o'clock, Adam took a deep breath and resolved to walk up The Mound toward Lawnmarket for a look-see. It was one of many streets that formed the city's ancient, cobbled backbone.

Tramping along the pavement, Adam felt miserably apart from the bustle and blare of life around him. He entered the tourist Mecca of the Royal Mile, where the courtyards, landmarks and souvenir shops were packed together as tightly as the people.

Picking a path through the crowds, Adam wondered what he was hoping to achieve. What was he going to do, knock on every door and hope he found the right place? And then what?

But suddenly, one face resolved itself from out of the crowd, scarred and heavyset, bobbing toward him. Adam felt like a sheet of ice had hardened over his chest in a single breath.

There was Frank Bateman, striding toward him.

17 LOST

(A) dam ducked down behind a trash can, pretending to tie his shoelace with shaking hands, his mind racing. Bateman, the man who'd pushed a gun to Adam's head and tried to slaughter Zed. He'd never wanted to see that big, scarred face again—nor that smug smile plastered all over it.

The stocky security man wore a gray raincoat over his dark suit, pressing his paunch through the crowds, a man on a mission. Adam held his breath as the big man strode closer. The street was full of people; Bateman wouldn't dare try anything here—would he?

A few seconds later, Bateman had pushed past his hiding place, heading toward the castle.

No, no, please, no. *Don't let him be the reason why*

Hayden hasn't shown, Adam thought in dismay. *Did Bateman follow me to Symtek and find out I'd asked Mr. Hayden for help?*

What's he done to him?

Adam dug his fingernails into his palms. He couldn't face being plunged back into the nightmare without even the hope of a helping hand. If Bateman *had* got Hayden, what could Adam do now?

Follow Bateman. He'll know where Dad is.

Even before the thought had fully formed, Adam was getting to his feet. He turned and started to follow the man's broad, gray back along the street.

Bateman ducked inside a narrow alleyway that led into a gloomy but well-tended courtyard, with ornamental urns ringing clean cobblestones. Adam watched the big man stride to his left, over to an old building studded with different shades of blackened brick, and climb the staircase to the door at the top.

Bateman knocked on the door. A petite black woman in gray trousers and a white roll-neck top opened up.

"Hey, Sammy," Bateman drawled loudly, as she stood aside to let him through.

"*She's* Sam Josephs?" Adam breathed, shrinking back into the cover of the alley. She looked so ordinary there on her doorstep, her straightened hair pulled back in a ponytail, holding a coffee mug in one hand. Someone you wouldn't look at twice. *That's how she gets away with doing what she does,* he supposed. *By not standing out.*

He watched Josephs take a swig from her mug. "Is our business taken care of?" she asked in a clear English accent.

"Smooth as clockwork. . . ." Bateman's gloating voice was bitten off by the slam of the door behind him.

Is it, now? Adam turned and retreated back down the alleyway. *I'll have to see what I can do about that.*

He turned back onto the main street, his mind racing. *Whatever Dad said, I've got to go to the police,* he thought. But if he did, what evidence could he show them? He'd given all the files to Hayden; they could be anywhere. . . .

I'll ask Zed, Adam decided, heading back down the winding slope of The Mound. *If he could sniff out an apartment in New Mexico all the way from Utah, maybe he can sniff out those files—before someone else grabs them.*

He broke into a run, feet slapping down hard on the pavement, arms like pistons jerking back and forth, hands karate-chopping the air. He cut a swathe through the armies of tourists, locals and festivalgoers who swarmed the city in search of amusement, barging people aside, ignoring the foul language thrown his way as he raced back to where he'd left his bike. There were plenty of people hanging out in the gothic shadow of the Scott Monument, and as he stopped for breath he couldn't resist a final, longing look to be certain that Hayden wasn't one of them, that he'd got the times wrong, that—

"Forget it," he muttered, turning his back on the monument and racing up St. David Street. But his way was blocked by a small mob of onlookers, gawping at the turning onto Rose Street opposite. There was an ambulance and a cop car parked there, and a group of policemen were standing outside one of the front doors and keeping back the curious crowds. *Maybe it's Hayden,* thought Adam, with a jolt. *He could have had an accident on his way here, or . . .*

He pushed past the morbid onlookers to see a pale young woman in bloodstained clothes being brought out on a stretcher by paramedics and eased into the back of an ambulance.

"Is she all right?" an old woman wondered.

"Blood loss, they say," a sharp-nosed man told her. "That and shock. Neighbor found her hiding under the bed, blood everywhere, babbling that she'd been attacked in the street and it was still after her."

Adam felt a smack of alarm. There were huge gouge marks in the wall beside the door. Marks that could have been made by giant claws.

The old dear sighed. "These kids nowadays, with their knives—"

"Kids?" The man smirked. "The girl said it was a dragon!"

"What?" Adam demanded, pushing his way forward.

"That's what she said," the man insisted, glancing at Adam. "I heard the police radio their station. A dragon that turned *invisible,* if you please. . . ."

The woman was wide-eyed. "It must have been the wild animal that escaped, the same one that killed those poor horses. It was on the news last night—torn apart, they were."

Adam turned and walked unsteadily back toward the bike racks in the square, a sick feeling building in his stomach as he remembered Zed's feverish behavior the night before, the blood on his lips this morning. . . .

So much for my last hope. Adam turned and ran back toward the square.

He wanted to keep running and never stop.

o   o   o

Zed's been ill, Adam reminded himself, pedaling hell for leather through the smart boxy terraces of Warriston on his bike. *He must have attacked that woman when he went out looking for water. . . .*

But a part of him wouldn't believe it. *Couldn't* believe it.

Maybe it was an accident, Adam decided. *If he'd wanted to kill someone, he would have, just like he did at Fort Ponil. He was killing anything that moved millions of years before the first humans came along.*

He thought of the huge gouge marks in the wall, gritted his teeth and pedaled harder, skimming past the traffic queuing to turn left onto the main road.

o o o

As he skidded to a halt on the stretch of weed-strewn concrete outside the warehouse, Adam braced himself for another confrontation. Zed had shown no sign of being violent that morning, but his mood swings seemed to be getting worse. Panting from his exertions, Adam approached the fire doors and pushed them open.

But the warehouse was dark and empty.

As his eyes grew accustomed to the gray light scattered through the filthy windows, he saw fresh markings on the wall. A chill plowed through him as he deciphered the letters gouged crudely into the old brickwork.

GET DAD NOW

"Oh, no. . . ." Adam rushed back to the fire doors, sent them crashing open. "Zed!" he screamed, staring wildly all around as the echoes cracked across the abandoned warehouse yard. "Zed, where are you? ZED!"

There was no sign of the dinosaur. No sign of any violence. Nothing. Adam sank to the ground, sweaty and exhausted from the mad ride over. Scared now half to death, his throat raw from shouting, he forced himself to calm down. "Reason it out," Adam muttered fiercely, just the kind of thing his dad would've told him.

Why would Zed have left a message? Was it a kind of warning, a declaration of triumph? Who knew how Zed's smashed-up mind worked?

"I'm not giving up on you, Dad," Adam promised. "Not till I've found you." The house in Lawnmarket had still been standing half an hour ago. But now . . . ?

Adam got up and retrieved his bike. He cycled away through the stiff breeze that was building, the bike's wheels bumping over the cracked concrete. As he pulled out onto the shore road he almost ran into a huge white truck coming the other way. *Steady*, he thought. *No use killing yourself.*

A shiver passed over him. *Not when there's a deranged dinosaur on the loose who can do it for you.*

o o o

The day passed for Adam in slow, exhausted confusion, wondering where Zed was, and what the message had meant. Most of all he wrestled with the question of what he was going to do now that Hayden had failed to show up.

He watched the Lawnmarket apartment for hours. Zed did not come calling, and no one else came or went. Adam even risked a trip to his own apartment. But nothing seemed to have changed since the last time he'd been there.

Midafternoon, in desperation, he cycled back to the BioQuarter and tried to get into Symtek.

"Mr. Hayden's still out," Megan informed him as soon as he came through the door.

"Could I wait for him in his office?" Adam asked hopefully.

She shook her head. "I'm sorry. Maybe you could try again tomorrow."

Adam decided to try again right now. "I, er, think I left something there, see. I had some files with me. . . ."

"There's nothing in the office. Mr. Hayden always clears his desk."

"Well, did he ask you to do any photocopying yesterday?"

"No."

Adam pressed his hands together. "Could I just check in there quickly? It's so important. Honest. You can even come with me. I might need to show what's in there to the police."

Megan's pretty face softened just a touch. "No exceptions, I'm afraid. We deal in highly sensitive data here—"

"I know. That's why your boss could be in big trouble," Adam told her, his frustration growing. "Look, if he doesn't come to work tomorrow, if you can't get hold of him, maybe you'll believe me then."

The hard mask came down again. "Would you go now, please?" Megan asked coldly.

"You don't understand how important this is!" Adam could hear how ridiculous he must sound but he couldn't help it. "First my dad went missing, now Mr. Hayden—"

"I don't want to have to call security," she interrupted, lifting the receiver.

"What if they're missing too?" Adam challenged her. Then, realizing he was getting nowhere with this approach, he turned and stormed out.

o o o

He sat on a bench and tried to cool down. The wind made it easier; it was gusty and stupidly cold for August.

Almost out of ideas now, Adam decided to try Mr. Hayden's address in St. Leonards. He checked it in his dad's phone. Though he didn't know anything about Hayden's family life, he decided he might as well call in—if he couldn't find the files, even if no one was home, he might at least find some clue as to what happened to him.

He cycled over, knowing this was about his final shot at getting something cast-iron to take to the police. Something they'd have to act on.

Hayden lived in a luxury town house on the edge of Holyrood Park. The barren sweep of the Salisbury Crags rose starkly from a steep slope of green, like fortified walls guarding Arthur's Seat beyond.

Adam tried the door but there was no reply. The place was shut up as tight as a tomb. He tried reaching in through the mailbox to get to the latch, but found it was hopeless.

How about a window, he thought. But a large metal casing high on the wall declared the place to be alarmed.

It was after nine o'clock by now, and the slow-falling night was painting the cliffs with ominous shadows. Sick of hanging around, Adam suddenly realized he'd eaten nothing all day. He spent the last of his money on a bag of chips from a convenience store, then cycled into a nearby park, carried his bike up a set of concrete steps and sat down in a quiet copse, chewing mechanically, trying to figure out his next move. There was no sound save for the wind rustling the leaves and distant dance music pumping from somewhere behind the tree line.

And then Adam heard an earth-shaking boom like thunder. Or like a bomb going off. "What the . . . ?" A sudden, distant gale of sound blew across the twilight, eerie and high-pitched. It reminded him of something. . . .

Like when you're at a theme park not far from

the really killer roller coaster, and everyone on it is screaming.

Alarm tingling across his skin, Adam scrambled toward the top of the rise to get a better view. Yes, it was definitely screaming he could hear, coming from the city center to the west. And as he staggered up, another thundering crash cracked apart the night around him.

He stood and gaped. And suddenly understood the screaming.

Because Edinburgh Castle was falling down.

Far across the rooftops, bathed in orange floodlights, that formidable, ancient pile was crumbling like chalk over the craggy ancient rock it stood upon. Adam flinched as a turret seemed to explode under two great impacts, a huge spray of debris arcing through the air. He watched, stunned and disbelieving, as history was demolished before his eyes.

A poisonous-looking cloud of dust was thickening in the orange lights. Through it, just for a second, Adam caught the barest details of a giant, dramatic shape sweeping through the air, barely visible unless you knew what you were looking for. A hunched, reptilian back. Vast wings extended. A thick tail smashing chunks from the battlements, deadly rain to crush the shrieking spectators who must be gathered below.

"Zed!" he screamed, as a bloodlusting bellow railed out into the night.

18 CARNAGE

An ancient wall bulged and bowed, then blew apart. Even from this distance, Adam flinched. It was like watching stone fireworks explode in the face of the on-looking crowds. A hollow rattle rose above the crumble of ruined stone—gunfire. There were soldiers at the castle for all the ceremonies. Perhaps a few had glimpsed that vast shimmer on the air, heard the exultant roar, and were trying to fight back.

The gunfire soon stopped, buried by still louder crashes.

And it's Zed, thought Adam. *He's cracked.*

He's killing.

The words GET DAD NOW rang in Adam's brain. He

grabbed his bike and set off for the road at a stumbling run. The castle was maybe a mile away. . . .

Reaching a wide, tree-lined avenue, he swung himself onto the seat and started pedaling. A police van streaked past, pursued by two fire engines, a deafening chorus of sirens. He passed people crowding together for comfort as they watched that indelible chunk of the skyline being clawed away. Helicopters swept overhead, making for the castle—police, film crews. Adam guessed that soon the skies would be thick with them. He crossed the road and took a left into a tall-walled canyon of buildings. Another police car bombed by, twinned with an ambulance this time. More helicopters buzzed above.

And a shadow fell over him.

The next instant, a car across the street buckled flat with a scrunch of steel as violent as any explosion. Adam swerved and lost control of his bike. He tumbled onto the pavement and slammed against a large, black salt bin. Winded, he turned, wide-eyed with fear.

Zed was striding toward him.

"Get back!" Adam shouted, cowering behind the bin. "Get away from me!"

But Zed smacked the huge plastic bin aside with a single swipe of his tail and lunged forward. His dark eyes were wild, his jaws flecked with foam.

Suddenly a woman's shriek, arrow-sharp, pierced the

night. A small crowd had gathered over on Nicolson Street, and they'd spotted the monster. Before Adam could react, Zed snatched him up and took off into the night sky, switching to chameleon mode so he seemed to vanish, a dark bruise moving over the face of the night.

"Put me down!" Adam hollered, struggling in the scaly crook of Zed's elbow. He saw the helicopters buzzing around the scene of destruction like wasps around jam. The traffic in the streets below was grid-locked. Honking horns fought for attention over the row of sirens.

Zed hurtled north over the darkened estates. He swooped down over an enormous large white truck parked outside the neighboring gasworks and landed near the warehouse with a thud, his claws churning up the old concrete. The distant bedlam of shouts, horns and air traffic carried even here to the dark, deserted wasteland, as Zed opened the roll-up doors and stalked inside.

Adam wriggled free of Zed's grip and dropped to the ground, shaking in the murky gloom. "You're crazy!" he yelled, staring up at Zed. "If you're gonna kill me, just get on with it!"

The creature seemed agitated, his claws clicking to-gether, padding around in a circle and scenting the air, his massive muscles tensed. Then he reached into his giant jaws and pulled something out.

It took Adam a few seconds to realize he was staring at a White Sox sweatshirt, crumpled and damp.

"That's Dad's," Adam said. He was frozen inside. "I got it for him in New Mexico. He packed it when he went to Fort Ponil."

"Dad . . . scent. Dad." He looked distressed, heaving great breaths. "Tried. *Get* Dad."

"Tried?" Adam breathed.

Zed nodded. "Get. Zed must. Must get."

"No!" Adam shook his head. "Smash all the castles you want, but for the last time, it's not him you should be after. You don't want to kill him!"

"KILL?" As he shouted the word, Zed thrust his huge face up close to Adam's. Adam gasped and lay very still, petrified as those huge, dripping teeth hovered just millimeters away from his neck. "GET. Get Dad." He stamped his foot. "Get. Dad. Out."

"Get him . . . *out*?" Adam felt a huge crash of confusion.

Zed's brows beetled together. "Pain. Dark. Get Dad out."

Adam stared at him. "That's why you came to our apartment in New Mexico?" Sadness, fear and relief surged through his brain in a dizzying rush. "You weren't trying to kill him? But you trashed the place!"

"Men. Guns," the dinosaur sneered. "Zed mad."

He's like an overgrown kid, Adam realized, still trembling. *Lashing out. Not thinking stuff through.* "Zed, why didn't you tell me this before?"

"Am . . . Ad . . . am." Zed stared down at him, just as he had back in Fort Ponil. "Zed. Ad. Knows."

"No." Adam shook his head. "No, you don't understand. You've got bits of my thoughts in your head, but I haven't got any of yours! I've never known what you were thinking about me, or my dad, or—"

"Dad," Zed growled. "Mine. Dad mine."

"*Your* dad?" Adam closed his eyes and thought. If Zed's head had been so scrambled he'd come to see Bill Adlar as a kind of surrogate father, and Adam as close to a brother, then no wonder he'd come so far to bring them back together. But what if Zed's mind was starting to heal, and the links binding him to Adam and Dad were breaking down? He remembered the way Zed had clutched his head in the horse field, thought of the woman being taken to the hospital, the castle collapsing. . . .

Zed's savage side had to be gaining control.

"What about Dad's shirt?" Adam said quietly. "Where'd you find it?"

"Long way. Sky."

Frowning, Adam spotted a string hanging down from the White Sox top with shreds of foil tied to the end. "Helium balloons," he whispered. "Someone tied his shirt to balloons and let them fly out over the sea?" He got up from the floor, thinking hard as more sirens went shrieking into the night beyond the warehouse grounds and the persistent helicopters whirled on overhead. "It was a trick, Zed. A trick to get you out of the way. Whoever did it knew you'd pick up the scent and try to follow. But why?" He looked imploringly at Zed. "The woman you attacked last night, did she have anything to do with Geneflow?"

Zed ignored him, sniffing the air. "Feel wrong. Bad."

"And what about the castle?" Adam demanded. "Zed, I know you're confused. You've been put through so much, but now you've—"

The dinosaur turned without warning and pounded over to the loading doors. He slammed his fist against the red button, almost tore it from the wall. The chains clanked as the metal barrier lifted.

"What is it?" Adam ran after him, afraid of what Zed might do next.

As he reached the exit, massive floodlights slammed on, the white light blinding. Zed flinched, ducked his head, while Adam threw his own hands up over his eyes. The growl of helicopters overhead grew louder.

"Hey, kid!" It was Bateman's voice, ringing out from the wall of light. "We're from the local pound, heard reports of a dangerous animal."

Before Adam could even react, Zed charged forward and stomp-kicked the nearest floodlights, buckling metal and shattering glass. He was about to follow up with the jab cross when a huge copter dropped from out of the darkness to drive him back. The rotor wash whipped at Adam's hair and clothes, forcing him to the ground. He saw there were men jammed in the doorway. Men with guns.

Zed roared out in defiance, flicked open his wings and turned himself invisible. But four jagged shafts of blue light spat from the men's weapons, and Adam was driven back by the fierce, crackling power. Zed's form reappeared as an outline of sparking, blinding energy, and his shrieks rose above the roar of the rotors.

Adam stared in horror, shaking his head. Wasn't this what he'd wanted—Zed under control, incapable of hurting anyone ever again? He looked away, unable to watch—and gasped as his arm was twisted up behind his back.

"There now, Ad—isn't this better?" Bateman had snuck around and grabbed him, hissing in his ear. "Thanks for leading us to him. Cycling away from Lawnmarket in such a hurry this morning. . . . You should've looked *behind* you instead of overhead."

Adam struggled wildly, gasping with pain, as the men kept blasting away. Zed was down on the ground, unable to withstand the assault, his head jerking from side to side. *They sent him on a wild-goose chase 'cause they wanted him tired,* Adam realized. *Wanted him easier to take.* "Mr. Bateman," he gasped, "his mind's all messed up, he doesn't know what he's done. Please, make them stop!"

"Stop? You know how hard it is to get private security for a gig like this?" Bateman laughed as the coils of blue energy thickened around the twitching dinosaur. "These guys are mercenaries. They want to be fighting wars." He twisted Adam's arm farther behind his back. "So, here's their war."

Zed tried to beat his wings, took a couple of stumbling steps, but then fell against the corner of the warehouse with a deafening crash. Masonry tumbled to the ground with him. He struggled feebly to rise.

"Wave two," Bateman shouted into a handheld radio. "Move in!"

The surviving floodlights dimmed as their operators, four more men in black, faces smeared with camouflage paint, ran forward with strange-looking pistols. They opened fire on Zed—no light show, just the eerie whistle and thud of silenced weapons, again and again. Behind them, the large white truck parked out in the road—the same one Adam had nearly crashed into earlier—was rumbling slowly toward the warehouse. The back doors were wide open, and men bearing heavy chains spilled out. *While we were away, these guys moved in,* he realized. The dinosaur lay motionless now in the blue spit of sparks.

"Get the ramps in place, and the forklifts," Bateman yelled to the men in the truck. "It's time we loaded up this scaly sack of—"

Adam brought his foot down hard on Bateman's ankle and elbowed the man in the stomach with all his strength. At the same time he wrenched himself free and sprinted, terrified, for the warehouse.

"Wave two, hold your fire!" Bateman bellowed. "Get the boy!"

The firing stopped as Adam disappeared into the loading bay. He ran for the fire exit, hoping to fool them into thinking he was still somewhere inside. But before he'd covered half the ground, the fire doors burst open. Two men carrying the weird pistols blocked his way. Adam skidded to a stop and in desperation ran for the humming power cables. Maybe he could ward them off with an electric shock, see how they liked their own medicine. . . .

He grabbed hold of the thick, snaking cable, straightened to face his attackers—and felt a thud in his chest. He looked down and saw some sort of dart protruding from his jacket, but couldn't feel a thing. Whimpering, he hefted the cable. A cold jolt went through his body like a physical blow. Adam fell over backward, the cable slipping from his grip. *We blew it, Zed,* he realized numbly. *Never got Dad out. They got us.*

The men rushed in, surrounding him like the darkness that was closing over his head.

19 CELLS

Adam stirred, his face cold and numb. There was a dull throb in the muscles of his left arm. He wished that could be numb too. Slowly he became aware of movement.

He realized his face was pressed up against glass. A car window? No, he was higher up in his seat than that. A truck, then. Big and heavy, by the growl of the engine.

Adam held very still. He didn't want anyone knowing he was awake.

It was dark outside.

Where am I?

The vehicle turned and Arthur's Seat swung obligingly into sight, massive in his window view.

He was still in Edinburgh. How long had he been out? The ugly scene at the warehouse stuttered through his head as a series of horrific images: Zed collapsing . . . Breaking free from Bateman's grip . . . Looking down to see the tranquilizer dart lodged in his chest . . .

Strange that the dart hadn't hurt. Adam looked down at his ghostly reflection in the glass and saw the end of it still sticking out from his jacket, like a syringe with a fluffy tail. And yet, it wasn't a sharp silver point he felt digging into his chest now.

He held his breath. *Dad's phone.* The dart must have hit that instead of his chest. So how come he had blacked out? He remembered the jolt that slammed through him as he'd tried to bring that unplugged cable to bear. . . .

That was it, Adam realized. He'd been shocked, not drugged, and no one had noticed the difference. And now he was awake, presumably earlier than intended, as his transport was still rumbling through the dark roads around Holyrood Park.

The truck grumbled into a gas station. No lights were on, but they turned left into a big shelter at the back, a car wash, maybe, or a service garage. *Maybe this is my chance to leg it,* he thought. *If I could only get outside somehow.*

Then the realization hit him: Where would he go? Where *could* he go to, all alone now? He was as much a prisoner of circumstance here as he'd been in New Mexico.

Maybe if Dad's here they'll let me see him.

The situation was taken out of his hands in any case. A few moments later, the ground lurched. They were going down into the darkness.

Adam kept faking sleep, but it wasn't so easy when you were descending into some creepy underground lair, eerily aglow with orange hazard lights. He wondered vaguely if he was still knocked out, if this was a dream.

The truck came to a halt in a large, rocky hangar. He heard a clamor of echoes—men's shouts, running footsteps, gruff bursts of two-way radio static, the piercing bleep of the truck's reversing sensors.

"Place the Z. rex in the holding pen." The female voice was English and cultivated—Josephs's voice. "I need to apply the brain sensors, so be quick. The tranquilizers won't keep it quiet forever."

Adam risked opening his eyes a crack to see the woman up close through the truck window. She was in her thirties maybe, barely taller than he was, slim and striking with smooth, dark skin. Her gaze held an unsettling intensity.

"We filmed everything that went down at the warehouse, Miss Josephs," one of the men said. "D'you want the tapes—"

"Drop them at my workstation," she snapped. "As for the boy . . . the tranquilizer should keep him out a while yet, but you'd better cuff him. Then leave him in the cell with Hayden."

So they did *get Hayden,* Adam thought. He looked down at the dart piercing his jacket, its tip embedded in the plastic shell of the phone. Perhaps there was some of the tranquilizer left inside—enough to use as a weapon?

Quickly, he pulled out the dart and slipped it into his jacket pocket. Then he shut his eyes as the truck door he was slumped against abruptly opened and he fell into the arms of some sweat-ape thug. The man wrestled him none too gently into some handcuffs and then carried him away.

Adam heard heavy doors grinding open somewhere behind him, more deep voices:

"I'm not going near that thing."

"The auto-loader will dump it for us. Get ready to pump in the tranquilizer gas."

At least Zed's alive, thought Adam. Then the sounds were swallowed up, as he was carried deeper into the cold, volcanic tunnels.

○　○　○

He wasn't sure how long the journey lasted, and though he tried to memorize the turns they were taking, he soon lost track. A heavy door squealed on its hinges, and he was laid down roughly inside. He gasped, unable to keep up the pretense of sleep any longer.

"Adam?"

As the door was closed and locked, he opened his eyes and found Mr. Hayden hovering over him, wild wisps of combed-over hair dancing about his pate. His suit and shirt were a bit crumpled, but otherwise he seemed well. The two of them were in a bare, rectangular room with rough stone walls, a table, a toilet and a single hard bunk. It felt like a prison cell.

Adam felt a rush of relief that he wasn't on his own. "Mr. Hayden! Have you seen my dad? Is he okay?"

"Josephs says he's just fine," Hayden assured him. "As fine as he can be, anyway. Sounds like he's cooperating."

"He is?" Adam tried to shrug off a stab of disappointment. "Cooperating on what?"

"So far as I can tell, Geneflow Solutions is developing a whole range of projects in facilities all over the world. But don't think badly of your dad. I'm sure he's only doing what he has to."

Adam nodded glumly and forced his thoughts away from that. "How did they get you?"

"I had a visit in the night. Took me by surprise, knocked me out cold." Hayden mimed being hit on the back of the head. "But, Adam, listen. This thing is massive. You know, we're inside a secret nuclear shelter, hidden under Arthur's Seat." He helped Adam rise.

"It was bought from the government by property developers in the 1990s hoping to turn it into a tourist attraction. But when that fell through . . . *they* stepped in."

"Geneflow Solutions?" Adam rubbed the back of his aching neck. "Who are they?"

"Geniuses, if the Z. rex project is anything to go by. I still don't believe they could pull off something like that." He looked hard at Adam. "But you do, don't you?"

Adam sighed. What was the point in holding out now? "I guess Josephs told you that Zed's been keeping me a prisoner, of a sort."

"Zed? That's your name for it?" Hayden raised his eyebrows. "So, you've spent time with the actual dinosaur?"

"Around twelve days," said Adam, with a strange feeling of pride. "Just him and me, pretty much."

"What patterns of behavior did you notice?" asked Hayden eagerly.

"Huh?"

"Sorry. I mean, did it display intelligence, or aggression, or . . . ?"

"Uh . . . he showed both, I guess." Adam took a deep breath. "When I first ran into him, he was really mad. Josephs had tried to burn his brains out. He killed some people—"

Hayden looked at him worriedly. "You had to wit-ness that?"

"It wasn't his fault," blurted Adam, surprising him-self. *Since when did I start sticking up for him?* "Zed was hurt, people were trying to kill him, and he fought back." Adam shuddered. "Fought back hard. But he was clever too. He actually defused a bomb—and set it again. Over here, he dug his way down to the electric-ity supply and ran power through to the old warehouse we stayed in."

"So it displayed real initiative!" Hayden seemed staggered. "That's incredible!"

"That's nothing," Adam went on. "He actually flew us across the ocean from America, all the way here. It took days and days, and after what he went through, I think it was all too much. He got sick—"

"Physical exhaustion can lead to lowered immune system functioning. But Zed could still communicate? Verbally?"

Adam wondered for a moment at Hayden's interest. *Dad would be the same,* he reminded himself, *if he heard something like this.* "Zed can speak a bit, read and write even. But like I said, his brain was hurt in New Mexico. He kind of lost his memory, and . . ." He trailed off, his head starting to spin. "Actually, *my* brain's not feeling too good."

"Must be the effects of the anesthetic wearing off."

Hayden perched on the edge of the bunk. "Sorry. I guess you expected an interrogation from the bad guys, not me!"

Adam forced a smile as the dizziness passed. "It's okay. I just wish I knew why they ever made a dinosaur. And so does Zed."

"Well, I can't tell you why," said Hayden. "But I think I can tell you *how*. Since it was my technology that kicked off the whole deal."

"Of course," Adam recalled. "When Josephs stole the blueprints of your bio-things. . . ."

Hayden nodded, looking pained. "Our bioregenerators release microscopic molecule machines into the patient's bloodstream. They work with the body to undo damage and replace it with healthy tissue. But in tests, we found our bioregenerators weren't only restoring damaged cells, they were *enhancing* them. Making them better than before! I found that, if stimulated correctly, the regenerators can even work on certain fossil remains."

Adam tried to look as though he had conversations like this every day. "Old bones and stuff?"

"The petrified remains of ancient animals. I thought—if I could only restore those ancient relics for proper study, think what we could learn. . . ." Hayden shook his head gravely. "But these people's ambitions ran far higher. And it seems they had access to actual soft tissue preserved at the heart of a T. rex femur recovered from hydrated sandstone in Wyoming some sixty-six million years old." He started to pace about the room. "Somehow they managed to make my molecule machines *fuse* with the dinosaur DNA. Instead of simply regenerating the original dinosaur design, they accelerated its potential evolution through millions and millions of years." He shook his head, marveling. "Brilliant. Extraordinarily brilliant."

Crazy, more like, thought Adam, uneasily. "But I thought dinosaurs evolved into birds," he said. "How come they didn't end up turning a T. rex into . . . I dunno, a chicken or something?"

"Evolution is the way in which a life form develops and adapts in response to changes in its environment," Hayden answered. "Something that happens naturally over millions of years. But there was nothing natural about what they did to those cells." He drew in a breath and let it out slowly. "I shudder to think what mutations they must have created in their first experiments. They were able to take control of the evolution process. Played a game of prehistoric 'What if?' by the sound of things. . . . What if the T. rex had grown wings that would carry him to fresh hunting grounds? What if he developed a kind of advanced chameleon skin, allowing him to blend in with his environment to creep up on prey?"

Adam joined in. "What if he could be made as smart as a human being?"

"Or smarter," Hayden shot back. "And he had four fingers and a thumb on each hand as we do, the better to shape his habitat?"

"You'd get the ultimate dinosaur," Adam murmured.

"The ultimate *predator*," Hayden corrected him. "A highly evolved, highly intelligent killing machine. Do you see now, Adam, why those papers you left with me are so vitally important? They contain information about how the bioregenerators can be applied in the different fields of biology." He leaned in urgently. "You're sure you don't have any more of these notes anywhere?"

Adam shook his head. "It's like I said—all the ones we took from New Mexico, I gave to you."

"And the others?"

"Buried in New Mexico. The lab there was blown up."

Hayden nodded, turned and paced toward the door, his wispy hair standing on end. "So, there's not a shred of evidence left, you say?"

Adam shook his head, frowning. Something felt wrong. "Um . . . no."

"Nothing that could incriminate these people or shed light on the process?"

"Nothing." Adam went suddenly very, very cold. "Mr. Hayden?" He swallowed hard. "You say you got hit on the head. Where, exactly? There's no mark."

Hayden turned slowly to face Adam. He smiled reassuringly. "It was the back of my neck they struck."

"And you said I felt bad 'cause the anesthetic they gave me was wearing off." Adam's heart was sinking and dragging every other organ with it. "If you were clobbered by these people, why would you think I was given an anesthetic?"

"Josephs told me, before you . . ." Hayden tailed off, and then sighed. "No, I shan't insult your intelligence. You're more astute than you appear, aren't you, Adam? A little of your father's analytical ability creeping into that young head, huh?"

Each soft-spoken word was like a nail thumped into Adam's chest. He found he could hardly speak. "What . . . what's going on?"

Hayden shrugged. "I guessed you were far more likely to speak honestly about the Z. rex's operational status and the existence of any further files if you trusted me. And I was right." He banged on the door of the cell; it swung open at once to reveal Frankie Bateman, standing impassively with a pistol aimed at Adam's chest.

Adam froze, his eyes hardening as he glared at Hayden. "You were never a prisoner here."

"That's right, Adam. I'm actually head jailer." Hayden gave him a regretful smile. "And if your dad causes me any further problems—you're dead."

20 SECRETS

For several seconds, Adam remained stunned by the sudden shift of events. Hayden had been tricking him right from the start. How could he ever have trusted this man? *Because Dad told me to,* he realized, *and because I needed to believe* someone *was on my side.* "You're in charge of Geneflow Solutions?" he asked finally.

"Let's just say I'm an influential figure," Hayden told him.

"But . . . I don't understand." Adam glanced at Bateman, saw the gun barrel, looked quickly away. "Your head of security over there tried to get me when I broke into my home, but blew it. How come you didn't just grab me when I came to your office?"

Hayden smiled. "That would hardly have suited our purpose. We had tried to contain and collect you in America, of course, but assumed you'd perished with the Z. rex when the bomb went off in New Mexico. A pity, we thought, since having your life in our hands gives us good leverage over your father." His green eyes were gleaming. "When Bateman sighted you outside your apartment, I was glad his attempt to capture you didn't work out."

"Sure you were," Adam muttered.

"No, really. When I found you in my offices, I guessed that the Z. rex must have brought you to Scotland," Hayden went on. "If we'd simply captured you at once, the creature would surely have come looking for you, as it did before—causing carnage and unwelcome attention. So we bided our time, employed a little trickery to put you off guard and followed you to learn where the Z. rex was hiding . . ." He grinned. "We picked up the two of you *and* the files you stole with little struggle and no loss of life. Works for me!"

Adam felt crushed inside, but he was determined not to show it to these maniacs. He squared his shoulders. "Where's my dad? I want to see him."

Even as he said the words, Samantha Josephs appeared beside Bateman in the doorway, silent as a shadow. "I've brought him," she announced.

"Adam?" It was his dad's voice, outside in the corridor. "Adam, is that—?"

"Dad!" Adam craned to see past Josephs and Bateman, his heart bunching up in his throat. "Dad, I'm here, I'm—"

The next moment, Bill Adlar pushed past them and flew to Adam, grabbing him in a bear hug. "Oh, Adam, they told me you were dead. . . ."

"I thought you were too," Adam whispered, his voice thick with the tears he was trying to keep down. "Thought I'd never see you again." For a moment the rest of the world faded away as he felt the solidity of his dad. "Have they hurt you?"

Mr. Adlar pulled away, and Adam was shocked to see how gaunt, how gray he looked. His glasses had been broken—they were held together with tape—and the rest of him looked to be in similar repair. "I'm fine," he said, convincing no one, a haunted look in his blue eyes. "But are *you* all right? Did Zed hurt you?"

Adam quickly shook his head.

"Josephs made us evacuate Fort Ponil when she found Zed was alive, thought he was out for revenge. To know I was leaving you . . ." Mr. Adlar wiped his eyes with the back of his hand, and took tight hold of Adam's arm. "When they said that you were alive, that you were here in Edinburgh, I didn't believe them at first, I thought it was another trick, a way to get me to—"

"It's okay, Dad." Adam felt a strange numbness settling over him. He'd waited so long to see his dad again, as though that would take the fear away and make everything seem better. Now he realized that wasn't going to happen; his dad was just as vulnerable as he was. They were trapped in this situation, both together.

"I'm sorry for all this, Adam," his dad murmured helplessly.

Hayden took a step forward. "Adam will be a lot sorrier, Bill, if you don't get on with the work with a little more enthusiasm."

"Should I demonstrate?" Bateman smiled at Adam, scratching idly at the healing scar across his cheek.

Mr. Adlar clutched Adam's wrist. "I can't perfect the Think-Send tech in the timescale you're working to, Jeff." His raw voice matched the look in his eyes. "However much you threaten Adam. Or me."

"Bill, I've been checking your progress," said Josephs. "The notes that we found in your apartment prove you've been duplicating much of your groundwork."

"Testing it properly," Mr. Adlar insisted.

Hayden shook his head. "Samantha has already performed the most thorough checks. I was paying her to do so even before you kicked her off your team."

Adam turned to his father in surprise. Mr. Adlar nodded. "Hayden's been building up to this for a long, long time, Adam. He and the rest of his would-be world changers in Geneflow Solutions."

"Dad, that night you came back after the meeting at Fort Ponil"—Adam looked him in the eye—"did you know what they wanted you to do?"

"Not for sure." His dad looked away. "But . . . I had an inkling."

"Then how could you get involved?" Adam demanded in confusion. "You must have known Josephs had stolen your research."

"Of course he did. But how could he resist?" Josephs looked at Adam, a faint smile on her face. "I told him my organization would fund the completion of Ultra-Reality—provided he joined the Z. rex project first."

"With yet another contract about to end, I guess I was clutching at straws. But I had no idea where the work was headed." Mr. Adlar turned to Hayden, his eyes hardening. "And until I was dragged into this crumbling hellhole, I had no idea you were behind any of it—'old friend.'"

"If you had, you would hardly have told Adam to go to me with the evidence you'd so clumsily compiled." Hayden flashed him a tight smile. "All right, Bill, now you've seen that we've got Adam and that he's unharmed. Why don't we all get back to work?"

Mr. Adlar went on glaring at him. "I want Adam to come with me."

"Oh, the boy's coming, don't you worry," said Hayden, in a tone of voice that suggested he should.

Adam gasped as Bateman yanked him roughly from

his dad's grip and steered him out of the cell into a featureless white corridor. From the clomping of footsteps behind him, he knew his dad, Hayden and Josephs were following close behind.

"What are you going to do with Zed?" Adam demanded.

"You should have destroyed that beast as I told you to, Bill," said Josephs curtly. "It would have been kinder."

"It would have been murder," Mr. Adlar shot back. "He's not an animal. He's intelligent, articulate. Self-aware. At least by lowering the voltage he had a shot at survival."

A jolt slammed through Adam's heart. "Then you *didn't* flick the switch to kill Zed, Dad. You did it to save him!"

"I had to try, Adam. I'm only sorry for all that my decision has put you through."

"And what about the good men I've lost to that thing, Adlar?" Bateman snarled. "Are you sorry for them?"

"Your good men simply weren't good enough, Mr. Bateman," said Hayden coolly, walking just ahead of Adam now. "They went rushing off to track the Z., and the Z. rex used its superior strength and skills to thwart them, ensuring its own survival." He smiled to himself. "That's the business of life, Mr. Bateman, and always has been."

"Yes, sir," said Bateman quietly. He yanked down

hard on Adam's arm to stop him walking, as Hayden marched up to a formidable set of sliding steel doors and pressed some buttons on a keypad. The heavy doors ground open with a whir of gears, and harsh white light spilled out from the huge room they guarded. From the looks of things, this was the underground control center of the aging nuclear shelter.

It was a strange mix of old and new. Whereas Fort Ponil boasted modern workstations, here the slimline PCs perched on old, ink-stained desks. As Bateman marched him inside and pushed him into a threadbare office chair, Adam noticed a large arc of metal studded with circuits leaning against the nearest desk—like a Think-Send headset only far bigger. At the back of the room, state-of-the-art computer servers hummed beside battered gray generators. Above them, four huge flat-screen TVs were pressed into the rock wall like dark windows, their chrome tops nudging rusted grilles. Each grille was festooned with fluttering ribbons to show that fresh air was circulating. With a chill, Adam saw the image of Zed's scaly bulk on one of the monitors. He was curled up in a rocky cell with sensor pads placed against his forehead, motionless and wreathed in white gas.

The holding pen, Adam thought.

Josephs crossed the room to sit at a workstation at the far side of the echoing chamber, close to another pair of enormous metal doors. The sheets of steel were pitted and scratched and stained with grease.

Adam wondered warily what they were designed to contain—or keep out.

"The place is a bit of a ragbag, I know," said Hayden, Bateman hovering by his side. "But research of this type costs a good deal, and sadly our resources aren't unlimited."

Adam pointed up at the screen. "So why try to kill Zed?"

"Because they screwed up." Adam's dad slumped into his chair and placed one hand on the oversized headset. "Sam put terabytes of knowledge into Zed's head using a variation of the Think-Send system. But she'd taken an early work in progress, full of glitches. The more information Zed absorbed, the more his mental state started to deteriorate."

Adam nodded grimly. "I guessed they must have brought you in to try and put things right."

Hayden looked across at Josephs, who shifted under his stare. "Talented and committed though Samantha is, for work so specialized I required the genius who first designed the system."

Mr. Adlar ignored the compliment. "They needed me to update the software and restore the balance in Zed's brain. I placed him in a simple Ultra-Reality scenario to focus his mind while I did so—but there were side effects." He paused. "I had to adapt the latest Think-Send system. As you know, it's patterned on your own brain waves—"

"I know, all right," Adam broke in. "Boy, do I know. And some of them got into *Zed's* brain, right?"

"Yes. He was in Ultra-Reality long enough to absorb traces of your own personality. When he came out, he was more headstrong, willful, even secretive at times." His dad smiled sadly. "Prone to sudden bad moods."

"Can't think why," Adam muttered.

"The traits of a *teenager*." Hayden pronounced the word like it was dirty. "Is it any wonder I ordered the creature destroyed? He was useless for my purposes."

"And if it really wanted to survive," said Bateman, "it should never have come after us."

"Zed didn't come after you for revenge," Adam said, "you just got in his way." He turned back to his father. "He came here to get you, Dad. Maybe 'cause he *did* pick up some of my personality, and I'd have come for you too. I guess Zed took me along 'cause in his head, me and him are linked."

"That partly explains the beast's motivation," Sam Josephs agreed, looking up from her monitor. "In the wake of the severe brain trauma we inflicted, the Z. rex could well have imagined a connection between the two of you. But it's not the whole story."

"Aha!" Hayden turned to her, expectantly. "You have the results from our brain scans of the Z. rex?"

"The tissue damage has healed even faster than you predicted," she said, and while her voice remained steady, her eyes were bright with excitement. "As you know, my first theory was that the Z. rex brought the boy here in order to kill him in front of Bill, and pay him back for his apparent betrayal."

Adam shook his head. "He wouldn't do that."

"Apparently not." Josephs gestured to Zed's image on the TV screen. "Those sensors have been feeding test images and information directly into the beast's brain. Pictures of itself and of other animals, along with footage we recorded at the warehouse tonight—"

Mr. Adlar broke in. "So, tell us your results."

"The Z. rex's physical-chemical reactions to you, Bill, are mixed. I'll need more time to go over them." Josephs looked at Adam. "But when it sees or hears the boy, levels of certain hormones increase . . . blood pressure rises . . ."

Adam scowled. "What's all that meant to mean?"

Josephs looked at him, a sardonic smile playing about her lips. "I believe that the poor, deluded creature has formed an affinity with you. Isn't that sweet? With all the time you've spent together, it has actually come to *care* about you. Like a brother."

Adam swallowed hard, groped about for words. None came.

"The one part of the equation that your science couldn't control, Hayden," Mr. Adlar said quietly. "Emotions. Spirit."

"You two are out of your minds." Bateman snorted. "Finer feelings in a dinosaur?"

"But this is fascinating!" Hayden cried, beaming. "What science can't control, it can still exploit, Bill. This is going to make for a most interesting experiment."

"Listen to yourself." Adam stared hatefully at Hayden. "Experiments! You don't give a toss about Zed and what you've done to him. Tricking him into flying away. Confusing him, *exhausting* him when he was already sick and hurting. It's all your fault that he went bad and out of control—"

"Bad?" With a sly look at Josephs, Hayden crossed to a bank of controls near the huge, grimy double doors. "Why, Adam, whatever can you mean?"

"You know he tore down the castle. He even attacked people!"

"How about that?" Bateman was shaking his head in some amusement. "The kid really fell for it, didn't he?"

Adam felt a prickle of unease. "What're you talking about?"

"Your precious Zed didn't hurt anyone here," said Hayden, a smile still playing about his mouth. "And I certainly won't allow him to take credit for the destruction of Edinburgh Castle." He turned to his controls and stabbed one with his finger. With an ominous clank and judder, the huge metal doors began to slide slowly open onto pitch-darkness. Adam saw that the color had drained from his dad's face, and he found himself holding his breath.

Then that same breath pushed out in a gasp as huge

chains clanked and scraped in the darkness beyond the doors, and the boom of giant footsteps slammed out a frightening rhythm.

The next moment, Zed appeared in the doorway, black eyes wild. His chops foamed with bloody froth that spilled down onto the massive metal collar clamped about his neck. The chain was at full reach, stopping him from entering the control room. He roared in frustration, an earsplitting crack of primeval thunder.

"Zed!" Adam shouted. "Zed, it's me, Adam! What have they done to you?"

Josephs shook her head. "This isn't your unstable friend."

Adam glanced up at the TV screen, his heart banging at the back of his throat. Zed was still lying in his pen, half hidden by gas.

"Say hello to Zed's clone, Adam." Hayden gazed up at the ravening monster with shining eyes. "Say hello to the *Y. rex*."

21 OPPORTUNITIES

(H)is clone? Like a twin?" Adam looked again between the drooling monstrosity before him and the identical dinosaur on the TV screen. "Then it was *this* thing that trashed the castle."

Mr. Adlar nodded. "The Y. rex was rapid-grown from Zed's regenerated cells."

"While Josephs and your dad salvaged what development work they could in New Mexico, I was leading the work on *this* project, here in Edinburgh." Hayden smiled, as the giant beast gibbered and gnashed his terrifying teeth. "I call him my Y. rex, because he's as close to his zenith as I will let him get. Much more of a *Yes*-dinosaur—uncontaminated by messy character traits."

As Adam looked into the Y. rex's blank, dark eyes, he knew in an instant that *this* was the monster he'd seen killing the horses in the field. Zed must have been lying ill back at the warehouse the whole time.

"Why?" His voice caught in his throat as he stared at Hayden. "Why did you make this thing destroy the castle?"

"Taking down a six-ton killer is likely to draw attention," said Josephs wryly, "unless something even bigger is happening on the other side of town."

Adam stared between her and Hayden in disbelief. "You had your pet monster destroy Edinburgh Castle as a *diversion*?"

"The chaos kept the emergency services fully focused on the Royal Mile," Josephs went on calmly. "Plus, the general clamor—and the presence of so many helicopters in the area—made it easier for our forces to approach the warehouse without alerting the Z. rex."

"You sound like you're reading the news or something!" Adam exploded. "How can you think you've got the right to pull something like this?"

"We *know* we've got the right," Josephs told him, her eyes dark and wide. "Superior power and vision *give* us the right."

"It was a very useful exercise," Hayden agreed, turning to Mr. Adlar. "Calm the Y. rex down, Bill. Now."

Mr. Adlar placed a slim metal keyboard beside the Think-Send headset and started typing. "This is why they need me," he explained to Adam. "The Z. rex has freedom of thought; he can respond to voice commands in any language, and access the data placed in his head whenever he needs to. But the mind of the Y. rex has been butchered—slaved to a series of computer implants. It doesn't understand human speech, only computer code uploaded using Think-Send."

Adam frowned. "You're going to fit that thing with the headset?"

"The Y. rex doesn't need to wear it," Josephs put in. "We're not taking the chance of your brain waves influencing it, as they did with Zed. So the headset connects to the computer first to filter out any trace of your personality."

"Then the computer sends the data directly to a receiver in Y's brain," Mr. Adlar concluded. He hit a button and a red LED glowed into life on the headset.

It's like you're controlling a character in a game, Adam realized, watching as the Y. rex started to raise and lower its arms and move its head from side to side in a grotesque parody of a dance. The repeated actions seemed to be soothing its wildness away. First one dinosaur, now two. . . . As he swung around to face Hayden, Adam felt as though he were losing his mind. "Why are you doing all this?" he asked helplessly. "Why dinosaurs? I mean, I know you're an expert on them, but—"

"Recreating and enhancing the most dangerous predator ever to roam the planet . . . that's a little splashier than cloning a sheep, wouldn't you say?" Hayden smiled. "Intelligence, imagination and sheer, unstoppable power, all in one package. When Y. rex and his army of brothers stand revealed, they will send a message to the world that Geneflow is not an organization to be trifled with."

"Army?" Adam echoed, splinters of ice prickling down his spine.

"Once the Y. rex is perfected, it'll be the template for hundreds of others," Josephs informed him. "Highly capable, precision-controlled, invisible agents of terror that we shall use to help achieve our ends."

Adam's blood was turning to liquid nitrogen in his veins. "No wonder Zed was able to work explosives and fly anywhere in the world."

Hayden smiled. "And such creations are simply a first step."

"A first step toward what?" said Mr. Adlar, turning from his computer screen now that the Y. rex had grown placid. "You and Sam keep hinting at experiments on other prehistoric creatures."

"What?" Adam felt his guts churn. "They're making *other* dinosaurs too?"

"Of course," said Josephs, as if this was the most natural thing in the world. "The techniques perfected in hyper-evolving the Z. rex can be applied to many other species, once viable DNA has been found."

Hayden nodded. "And each will play its part in Geneflow's grand design."

Mr. Adlar raised his eyebrows. "Which is?"

"What d'you think this is, Bill—*Scooby-Doo*?" Hayden smiled without humor. "Why should I reveal all our plans to a meddling kid and his stalling father?"

Adam's dad stood up angrily. "I have a right to know how my work is going to be used!"

Josephs raised her voice too. "If you had one iota of vision, you'd have grasped the possibilities long ago."

"Exactly." Hayden stared at Mr. Adlar. "Do you seriously think I'm going to stop at reimagining dinosaurs, Bill? Think of all the potential we have as a species. Potential we're never going to reach because we're too busy destroying the planet. Destroying *ourselves*."

Mr. Adlar met his gaze grimly. "You have an alternative?"

"By comparing the cells of an ancient T. rex with those of its closest living relatives today, we understand the ways in which genes develop over millions of years. And if we apply that understanding to human cells and evolution—"

"Dad?" Adam chewed his dry lip. "What is he talking about?"

Mr. Adlar let out a heavy breath. "He wants to play God."

"Science is the new god, Bill," Hayden said softly. "Science is the creator now." He walked over to join

Josephs at her workstation. "But the details don't concern you. All that's for the future."

"There's still a long way to go till your perfect Y. rex prototype is ready, Jeff." Mr. Adlar didn't try to keep the satisfaction from his voice as he turned back to Adam. "Its savage nature means it constantly fights against the programming. It's abandoned several training missions partway through to go AWOL around Edinburgh—hunting animals, even attacking people—"

"We're regaining control over it faster each time," Josephs protested.

"And I'm sure you'll solve the problems completely now that your son is here, Bill," said Hayden. "If you don't, Mr. Bateman will just have to hurt him very badly."

Bateman nodded impassively. "Anytime you say, Mr. Hayden."

Mr. Adlar looked helplessly at Adam. Adam turned away, unable to meet his stare. *And I thought I was scared before*. He felt for the tranquilizer dart in his pocket, tempted simply to jab it into his thigh, put himself to sleep and hope he stayed that way for a long, long time. He'd got caught, so now his dad would have no choice but to help these maniacs. He looked up at Zed on the screen, still lying prone in the fog-wreathed room. If there was only some way he could be freed. . . .

"Open Y's mouth, Bill," said Hayden. "We lost contact toward the end of his spree. Let's see how much of his payload he deployed."

Mr. Adlar tapped on the keyboard. The Y. rex jerked into life, reached into its mouth and pulled out—

"A bomb," Adam breathed; it looked just like the one back at Fort Ponil.

"The Zenithsaurus was designed with special pouches in the lining of its mouth," said Josephs proudly. "So it can store tools and equipment inside for sabotage missions."

"But it planted only three of the bombs at the castle before the programming slipped." Hayden resumed his pacing. "I thought a programmable beast with no imagination would prove more reliable than one that could think for itself. But Adam's experiences with the Z. rex suggest an ability to improvise that could serve it well on terror missions." He nodded thoughtfully. "You know, I think it's time for a face-off."

Adam frowned. "A *what*?"

Hayden turned calmly to Josephs. "Sam, would you arrange for the Z. rex to be disconnected from the sensors, given a stimulant shot and transported to the Ring, please?"

Without hesitation, she picked up the phone on her desk and started giving instructions to whoever was on the other end.

"Dad?" Adam said.

"The Ring is a giant cavern where the Y. rex is trained

and exercised," Mr. Adlar explained, his attention fixed on Hayden. "Jeff, you can't be serious about letting Zed and Y clash in there. They could kill each other."

Hayden shook his head. "If there's no clear victor, we'll simply flood the Ring with tranq gas. That'll finish the fight."

Adam shuddered, as visions of the Y. rex hunting the horses flashed into his mind. "But you can't *make* Zed fight that thing!"

"I'm betting I can make him do anything," said Hayden, "just by threatening your life."

"No," Mr. Adlar protested. "I'm doing as you ask, what more do you—"

"You heard Samantha, Bill. The Z. rex cares about Adam. That's one lovable kid you got there." Hayden's voice hardened. "I told you—what science can't control, it can still exploit. Those two creatures are exactly matched physically. Only their minds are different." He smiled at Josephs. "Here we have the perfect opportunity to study the pros and cons of free will versus expert control . . . and whatever the outcome, whoever has to die—we're going to take it."

22 BATTLE GROUND

(A)dam sat slumped in his chair, his wrists throbbing from the chafing handcuffs, all but forgotten by everyone as the preparations for the battle between Y and Zed intensified.

Sam Josephs worked quietly and calmly at her workstation, apparently unbothered by being so close to the huge metal doors and the Y. rex framed between them like a scaly statue. Her movements at her computer were so precise that she could've been under remote control herself.

Adam looked at his haggard father, poring over the command translator log. Now and again, Josephs would come over to confer about something.

This is all my fault, Zed, Adam thought miserably. *I got myself caught. I got* you *caught. And I'm so, so sorry.*

All four of the big screens on the wall were switched on now. One showed the empty pen while the others showed a fierce swarm of static. What sights would soon be cutting across the glass?

There was a squawk from Bateman's radio. "The monster's parked up outside Ring West Entrance. We're ready for loading."

"About time," Bateman drawled, and glanced across at Josephs. "Sammy baby, your big scaly Z-failure is good to go, west side. You want to let it in?"

Josephs didn't reply, but walked calmly to the bank of controls beside the Y. rex. Hayden had already worked the door to its pen from here, and now she touched another button in the same row—presumably opening the west entrance to the Ring.

"Loading now," came the voice on the radio.

Just then, Hayden breezed into the lab, waving a big bag of cookies and a steaming jug of black, bitter-smelling coffee. "Gingersnap, anyone?" he called, flipping one over to Bateman, who caught it one-handed. He offered another to Josephs, who shook her head. "That's good, I've got to make them last. They come from that shop near the castle, and I do believe there's a bit of a flap on out there." Bateman chuckled, and Josephs smiled wanly. Adam and his dad swapped anxious looks. "Who's for fresh coffee? I want everyone awake for this."

"Y's been primed with over a hundred attack strategies as well as sixty defensive maneuvers," Josephs announced.

"Excellent." Hayden poured Mr. Adlar a scalding hot cup of black coffee. "Doesn't this beat animating hollow video game characters, Bill?"

Adam's dad took his coffee without a word.

"Just remember, if it takes too long to select one of your programmed attack strategies at any point in the contest, you choose for it," Hayden instructed. He crossed to stand beside Adam, who was slumped in his chair. "And make sure you keep the Y. rex's stress levels in check, Bill. It's no kind of test if Y beats Z by shrugging off our control and going beserk. If you let that happen"—Hayden let some boiling hot coffee spill on the back of Adam's cuffed hand. Adam gasped with pain.

"All right," Mr. Adlar said angrily, hitting buttons on the adapted Think-Send headset. "Point taken." He turned his attention to the screen.

Fuming and frightened, Adam tried to shake off the burning liquid, wiped his hand on his jacket—and again, his fingers brushed against the dart in his pocket, felt the sharp tip through the thick cotton. *There has to be something I can do. . . .*

"Sam," said Hayden brightly, "is Y good to go?"

"He's good." She nodded to Adam's dad, who pressed a couple of function keys on the steel keyboard.

"Restraint collar removed," Josephs reported.

At once, the Y. rex jerked into life, turned and stamped away from mission control, vanishing from sight down a rocky tunnel. Adam saw that a small window on his dad's monitor was showing a hazy, lurching view of the tunnel. *Think-Send is letting Dad see through Y's eyes,* he marveled. *So he can help it choose what to do.*

Josephs got up, flicked a switch on her console and the heavy metal doors to its pen ground slowly shut. "Y is on its way to the Ring."

Bateman smirked. "Going off to war like a good soldier."

"I'll be monitoring its vital signs and body chemistry at all times," Josephs went on. "If it looks like it's shaking off control . . ."

"Bill will get straight on the case," Hayden concluded. "That is, if he knows what's good for his son."

Adam's dad tensed his shoulders, but did not turn around.

"Now, I want everything recorded," Hayden announced. "Mr. Bateman, you're in charge of audiovisual."

"Got it." Bateman nodded, crossed to a kind of mixing desk on the table behind Josephs and started hitting buttons.

The large monitors on the wall flickered. Then Adam found himself staring up at the image of a rocky cavern spread across all four screens, lit up with dramatic spotlights like some cheesy tourist attraction. *The Ring,* he thought. It was a massive space. In the center, a large, familiar figure lay sprawled on the ground.

Zed.

Hayden swigged his coffee. "Check cameras, Mr. Bateman."

Bateman flicked switches. The image on the screens changed, still showing the Ring but flitting between different angles—from above, from the side, from every possible perspective. Adam saw two large doors on either side of the Ring—the west access point that Zed must have come through, and one other to the east.

"All cameras functioning," Bateman announced, index finger riding a fader. "Zooming in."

One camera crash-zoomed in on Zed's slumped form. Even in sleep, the scaly face was set in a savage sneer. Adam felt his pounding heart inch slowly up his throat.

"Send the Y. rex into the antechamber," said Hayden, crossing to join Bateman beside the mixing desk. "Time to test the radio link, I think. . . ." He leaned closer to a small built-in microphone. "Testing. Z. rex, do you hear me in there?" The words echoed from the vast plasma screens a second or so after he spoke. "I repeat: Z. rex, do you hear me?"

The dinosaur's dark beady eyes flickered open. "Zed hear."

"Are you all right, Zed?" Adam couldn't help himself. "It's me!"

"There's no need to shout." Hayden nodded to Bateman, who fetched Adam and dragged him closer to the microphone. "We *want* the Z. rex to know we've got you."

"He knows," Bateman murmured. On the screens, Zed clamored heavily to his feet and started looking about anxiously. He shifted from foot to foot. "Ad . . . am?" he grunted. "Where?"

Hayden took a swig of coffee and smacked his lips. "Hit the doors."

Josephs flicked another switch on the console that stood beside Y's holding pen. Then she hurried back to her workstation. A distant rumble carried through the rock floor as the Ring's East Access doors began to open.

Adam stared helplessly as white brightness from beyond spilled into the Ring. He saw Zed slowly straighten as the shadow of his opponent fell over him, eating away the light.

The Y. rex's roar bellowed from the monitors, distorting every speaker. At the audiovisual rig, Bateman nudged down the volume.

Zed reacted to the vast figure as it stamped into the Ring. "Zed," he growled, bewildered. *"Me."*

He was cut off by a vicious howl and the hissing swipe of claws. There was a scuffle of heavy footfalls.

Zed roared in return, a deep, bestial sound of anger. Or maybe fear. Adam realized Zed would wonder at the sight of his twin, try to reason out what was happening. His clone, on the other hand, would simply see an enemy to be killed.

"No!" Zed rumbled. "Not. Fight."

"Zed, get away from that thing!" Adam shouted helplessly.

"Good advice." Bateman smirked. "Where's he going to go?"

"Kill your opponent, Z. rex," Hayden instructed. "If you don't, it shall kill you. And then it will kill your friend Adam."

"Ad . . . am?" Zed growled as the Y. rex took a threatening step toward it.

"Y's testosterone levels are increasing too fast," Josephs reported. "There's a lot of adrenaline. Bring it down, Bill."

Adam's dad was typing frantically. "I'm telling its brain to produce more stress inhibitors."

"Don't calm it too much," called Hayden.

"Zed, it's gonna be distracted in a few seconds!" Adam yelled desperately. "If you hit him hard enough—"

Hayden nodded at Bateman, who quickly struck Adam across the temple with the back of his fat hand.

Adam cried out, the force knocking him to the floor as Zed bellowed in anger. He saw his dad rise angrily in protest, but Hayden stabbed out with his finger. "Sit *down,* Bill," he thundered. "Do your job—or I'll let Bateman really go to town on him."

Adam lay curled up on his knees, pretending to be hurt worse than he was, reaching with some difficulty for the dart in his pocket. If Bateman came at him again . . .

But the big man was back watching the screens, as was Hayden. Josephs and Mr. Adlar were poised at their stations as if playing some sick multiplayer video game. Adam was forgotten already.

"Implement attack strategy seven," called Josephs.

Another roar boomed over the flat screens. The Y. rex aimed a slicing blow at Zed's head. Zed ducked aside—but as he did so, Y turned and lashed out its tail, just as Zed had done to Sedona back in New Mexico. The thick, powerful tip caught Zed under the chin, smashing his head back. He staggered and fell to the ground with a rasping croak, and the Y. rex howled exultantly.

"Attack strategy seven successful," Mr. Adlar called back in a flat monotone.

"Get up," whispered Adam, glued to the screen. "Please, get up."

Zed tried to rise, but his mirror image lashed out

with its fist, smashing him in the jaw. Blood and teeth spat from Zed's mouth, an explosion of crimson and ivory. Adam's guts twisted as the Y. rex howled again, teeth quivering, eyes narrowed to slits.

The creature pounced, and Zed went down beneath the mountain of scaly, sinewy flesh. All four screens erupted in a dark green frenzy of tangled limbs and gleaming claws.

"Come on!" Bateman sounded like he was cheering on a boxer in a prize bout. "Stuff it to him!"

"I still don't like those adrenaline levels." Josephs frowned at her screen. "This is the point we lost Y in the castle attack."

"The next few seconds are crucial," said Hayden. "You selected an attack strategy, which the Y. rex implemented. Now he should select one of his own."

"I thought you didn't want that thing to have free will," Adam called out shakily.

"He's free to select from the options *I* have given him," Hayden snapped. "That's not thinking for himself."

One of the giant, flailing reptiles broke free of the other's grip and rolled clear. Adam saw by the bleeding jaw and the missing teeth that it was Zed. But already the Y. rex was back on its feet and coming at him once more. Zed launched himself into the air, flicked out his wings and soared up toward the vaulted ceiling like some nightmarish dragon.

"There's nowhere to go, freak," Bateman said with delight.

The Y. rex roared angrily at Zed as he circled above just out of reach.

"Still not selecting a fight strategy," called Josephs.

Hayden's eyes never left the screen. "Give it another five seconds."

Zed, meantime, was making full use of the delay. He suddenly banked left and attacked part of the wall, shearing through solid rock with his talons to expose thick cables that ran like arteries beneath.

"The environment controls!" Josephs leaped from her chair like a jack-in-the-box. "If he destroys them, the Ring safeguards go down."

"Get away from there," Hayden shouted into the microphone, "or I'll kill Adam now." But the threat was unnecessary. The Y. rex had chosen his move and slammed into Zed just as he tore through one of the shielded cables. The lights flickered. Both dinosaurs blazed blue for a moment, then broke apart and spiraled to the ground.

"Some damage to nonessential systems," Josephs reported tersely.

Bateman had turned to check another bank of controls. "I think the gas pumps have gone off-line. Now we can't tranq the beasts if things get out of hand."

"So, get your men to stand by with the shock-guns,"

Hayden told him, with a meaningful glance at Mr. Adlar. "Not that it will come to that. Right, Bill?"

Bateman gave the order into his radio. A deep voice responded, shot through with static. "Copy that. Standing by."

Adam hardly heard them, glued to the struggle on the screen. Y. rex lunged for Zed's wing, tearing into it like a chewy steak. Zed shrieked with pain and fury, slicing at his twin's scaly back with carving-knife claws. Y retreated for the first time, blood flooding from its wounds.

"That one hurt," Josephs shouted, her dark skin glistening with sweat. "Huge production of glucocorticoids."

Bateman glanced at her. "Huh?"

"It's scared," Hayden translated. "Reinforce the programming, Bill. We've got to spike Y. rex back into attack mode."

Adam held his breath, willing Zed to resume the attack while he could. A close-up of Zed's face filled one of the four screens as he waited uncertainly, wings tightly folded now, watching his twin. His eyes looked pained, almost sad.

Suddenly, Zed seemed to notice the camera. "STOP FIGHT!" he roared, stomping toward it. His open jaws filled the screen. The image went dead. Bateman quickly patched in another security camera to replace it. Zed roared again. "Not! Fight!"

Hayden pressed his lips to the microphone. "You've got no choice, Zed."

"Y's fear levels receding," Josephs shouted. "You're doing it, Bill."

"Don't, Dad," Adam whispered as the Y. rex launched into flight and screamed across the Ring at Zed, claws outstretched. "Please."

"It's gone to strategy thirteen!" called Josephs. "Full charge with talon attack."

"Did you choose that strategy for him, Bill?" Hayden demanded.

Mr. Adlar shook his head wearily. "Y did it by himself."

Hayden smiled.

There was a sickening smack as Zed's body was crushed against the rock wall. Y. rex grabbed Zed's injured wing with both claws, twisting the thick, gristly sail of skin like he was wringing out a dishcloth.

"Yes . . . a definite follow-through," said Josephs, excitement building in her voice. "It's working through the close-quarters combat strategies in order." She went on with her commentary, unmoved as Zed howled and slipped in his own blood, trying to wrench himself free.

Adam bit his lip, shocked by the violence. *Come on,* he willed Zed. *Break free, you've got to!* Finally, Zed managed to loop his tail around his twin's neck and yank down hard. The clone fell flailing onto its back.

Zed raised one foot to stamp down on Y's neck—then seemed to hesitate.

It was a mistake.

Y jammed a handful of claws into the underside of Zed's foot, slashing his sole, driving him back.

Bateman gave a pantomime wince. "That's gotta sting."

"Strategy nineteen!" Josephs cried. "Y. rex is self-selecting from the range of options."

"The programming is holding!" Hayden drained his coffee in a flamboyant gulp. "We're doing it, people!"

And Zed's losing. Adam could see the cloudiness in those dark eyes, where teeth, tranqs and shock-guns had taken their toll. He eyed the battered old watch on his dad's wrist ticking away each sickening second of the conflict.

And suddenly, Adam knew what he had to do. He'd have just one chance.

With a roar like a freight train tearing past the sidings, Y. rex hurled itself at Zed. A frenzied soundtrack of grunts and thumps ensued, a pounding, haphazard rhythm like a wild heartbeat going into arrest. Mr. Adlar glanced over at Adam and saw what he was holding. He caught the look in his son's eyes.

"Willful, you called me, Dad. And secretive." Adam sprang toward his father and brought the dart plunging down. "And in the mother of all bad moods!"

Mr. Adlar gasped and clutched his wrist.

Hayden spun around from watching the screens. "What the—?"

"I drugged my dad just like you tried to drug me," Adam shouted, his own adrenaline levels going through the roof as he held up the tranquilizer dart to Bateman. "Now he can't help your Y. rex stay in control!"

Bateman jumped up. "How did you—?"

Adam hurled the spent dart at the big man's feet. "Your mercenaries shot this at me in the warehouse, but it never went in."

Mr. Adlar collapsed, sprawling across the computer keyboard. Josephs looked over in alarm. "Don't take your eyes off that display, Sam!" Hayden bellowed. "Mr. Bateman—"

"On to it," Bateman lowered his head and charged at Adam.

"Not him!" Hayden yelled. "See to Bill. We've got to revive him!"

Bateman hesitated midcharge—and Adam grabbed the moment. He hurled himself into his creaking office chair with every ounce of strength he had, gripping the low back with his cuffed hands as he rode it out of the security head's path and headed through a canyon of desks straight for Josephs. She looked up at the last moment, just as Adam crashed into her, shoving her from her seat. She fell awkwardly, cracking the back of her head on the edge of the audiovisual console behind her.

She didn't get up again.

Too scared to feel even a second's satisfaction, Adam started to stab at every button on the console. "Zed!" he shouted, and heard his own voice ring back at him over the flat screens with a squeal of feedback. "Make it angry and it'll lose control! It can't think like you can."

Hayden looked livid, already sprinting toward Adam. Bateman was just behind him.

Oh, God, oh, God. Adam grabbed Josephs's mug of coffee with both cuffed hands and chucked it at Hayden. Hayden ducked down; the mug sailed past him. He kept on coming. In desperation, Adam lifted a metal clipboard from the desk and swiped wildly at Hayden's head. This time, he connected. As Hayden staggered back, blocking Bateman's own attack for a moment, Adam scrambled over Josephs's desk to reach the console that worked the doors. He flicked every switch he could see. The double doors ahead of him started to grind open; the dark pen beyond breathed the stink of reptile and rotting meat into the room. An escape route? No, Bateman was still coming. He would shut the doors, shut Adam's eyes forever unless . . .

Adam joined his fists, took a clumsy swing at Bateman and missed. Bateman thumped him in the stomach. The breath exploded from Adam's lungs and he doubled up, falling to the floor. On the screens, Zed was on his belly, frantically crawling, dragging Y. rex behind him. Y's jaws were clamped around Zed's tail, brutally scissoring the tough flesh.

Get out, Zed, Adam willed him, *just get away*. Then Bateman stepped over him, blocking his view. Still struggling for breath, Adam watched the big, sneering man draw back his fist, a slow and measured movement—like a blunt arrow being readied for flight. Zed's roar of pain and fury rattled the speakers and tears blurred Adam's view as the fist hurtled down toward his face.

23 KILLING

(T)here was a booming crack—as Bateman's fist hit the floor and the rest of him followed in a crumpled heap.

Adam wiped his eyes. His dad was standing over him now, wielding the Think-Send keyboard in shaking hands. He chucked it away and scooped up Adam into his arms.

Feeling sick with relief and about a hundred miles tall, Adam pressed his head against his father's chest. "My dad, the action hero."

Mr. Adlar pulled away, squeezed his arms. "Very clever, bringing that dart down on my watch strap. Seemed to fool the others."

"Dad, look!" Adam pointed up to the monitor screens with a jolt of excitement. The Y. rex had started moving its arms up and down again and shaking its head, the "calm-down" routine Adam had seen earlier. And rather than press home his advantage, the wounded Zed was scrabbling at the heavy doors blocking the west exit with bloodied claws.

"I put Y out of attack mode," said Mr. Adlar, studying the switches on the door console. He jabbed one, and both doors to the Ring began to crank slowly open. "I don't know how long it'll remain harmless but—"

"What have you done?" Hayden, a blackening bruise on his forehead, struggled up, stumbled over Josephs's fallen body and started hammering at her computer keyboard. "You just killed your son, Bill. I hope you know that. The Y. rex will—"

"I'm sick of your threats, Jeff," Adam's dad shouted. "I won't be your prisoner a minute longer." He started forward to confront Hayden—but Bateman had stirred and made a grab for his ankle. Adam quickly kicked Bateman's wrist away before he could make contact. Seeing the danger, Adam's dad retreated back to the door console and yanked a cable from the back of the unit. Sparks spat from the metal housing. "That'll jam the doors. Come on, Adam."

"How far d'you think you'll get?" Hayden screamed after them.

Mr. Adlar didn't answer as Adam followed him into the fetid darkness of Y. rex's pen. Hayden's voice echoed weirdly after them: "All security to the Ring, west exit. Doors jammed open—proceed with caution. Eliminate anyone and anything that tries to leave."

Adam stepped carefully over the shattered rib cage of some long-dead animal. "Does this tunnel lead anywhere else?"

"Only to the Ring. So we've got to be fast." His dad led the way through the passage. "Y. rex is liable to snap out of the trance at any moment—bleeding, sore and very, very angry." He looked seriously at Adam. "Zed is our one hope now for getting out of here."

Wading through the gloom they reached an archway in the back of the wall guarded by a huge, half-raised door. The dented steel was scored with deep scratches. Adam shuddered as he ducked down beneath it and into another huge tunnel, just like the one in Fort Ponil. His heart felt tight as a drum. He was sure he could hear scuffling behind them. Bateman? Guards? Maybe even Hayden himself. . . .

His dad caught his hand and squeezed it. "It's okay, Ad. We're going to get out of here."

"You honestly think that?" Adam squeezed his hand back and pulled away. "You don't have to treat me like a kid, Dad."

"Maybe if I'd remembered you *were* a kid instead of treating you like luggage to carry around with me, we wouldn't be in this mess now, huh?" Mr. Adlar sighed. "I am unbelievably proud of you, you know that? I should have told you more often."

Adam looked at him. "Now you're sounding like you really *don't* think we're going to get out of here."

His dad's only answer was a wry smile. Adam smiled back and stayed close to him. Somehow, the silence between them felt more comfortable now.

They moved quickly, quietly into a smaller cave, studded with bright spotlights. "This antechamber is where Y. rex is inspected for damage after missions," Mr. Adlar explained. "The Ring's straight ahead."

"And so are Bateman's mercenaries." Adam tensed up as he heard the sudden blast of shock-guns and the crack of bullets. "They must be finishing off Zed. He's hurt already, he won't be able to—"

A soft, broken whining sounded from up ahead.

"Zed?" Adam broke away from his dad, ran through into the arena—and almost collided with the bloody, slobbering chops of a fallen dinosaur. His heart lurched—this was not Zed, but the Y. rex. It still had all its teeth, and the wounds on its neck caused by Zed's raking claws were still bubbling blood. The scaly eyelids were screwed up tight, and claws and tail were twitching in time to the rattle of the gunfire, as though it were having bad dreams.

"It's already throwing off the programming," Adam's dad muttered, running up behind him. "It may be hurt, but will be blood-crazed, unstoppable. We have to be quick."

Adam started to make for the gaping metal mouth in

the wall opposite, the west exit. "Zed must be through there."

"Easy, Adam," his dad held him back. "Zed can stand up to a firefight better than we can."

"And now I get to prove it!" shouted Bateman from behind them.

Adam's heart catapulted against his ribs. He whirled around to find the big man's paunchy silhouette in the well-lit antechamber.

"Hayden told me to shoot to wound," Bateman went on, raising his gun. "Although, frankly, the way I'm feeling right now—"

But the rest of the threat was lost in a deep, earsplitting shriek. Y. rex must have snapped out of its trance and seen the human intruders. It lunged for Adam, long neck outstretched, jaws snapping. Mr. Adlar saw it coming and shoved his son clear—just as Bateman's gun spat thunder. Adam heard a whistle of air as the great jaws swung shut and a blast of foul breath broke over him. Bateman cried out as Y's flailing tail smashed his legs from under him and sent him crashing into Mr. Adlar. The two men went tumbling across the arena, their twisted limbs intertwined.

"Dad!" Adam yelled, backing away from the Y. rex on all fours. The drooling monster watched him with cold, crocodile eyes. The pits of its nostrils twitched. It snapped its jaws and scraped its claws together like some hideous butcher sharpening his knives. Roaring like a thousand tigers, Y. rex prepared to pounce, corded muscles twitching and dancing under its reptilian skin.

"No . . . *no* . . ." Adam screamed as that twisted, inhuman face came flying forward to devour him—

Only to crunch against a wall of solid, scaly flesh instead, as a huge figure dived forward protectively.

"Zed!" Adam gasped.

The Z. rex kicked Y's face aside with savage force and followed it up with a blow from his bloodied tail that clubbed the beast to the floor. Crimson saliva dripped from his swollen, gap-toothed jaws as he sliced through the chain that joined Adam's handcuffs with one claw.

Adam stared up at him. "I . . . I'm glad you're okay."

"Get . . . Dad," Zed panted. "Go."

Glancing back at the west exit, Adam swore. "More guards!"

Zed pounded back toward the entrance where three men had appeared, shock-guns aimed to fire. Within seconds, Zed was engulfed in a storm of blue light, snarling and snapping with pain. But he kept on going, staggering to the side of the huge metal doors. Grunting with effort, his whole body shaking, he scored his claws down a seam of cement to expose copper piping, then twisted it away from the wall. Steaming hot water came spurting out under pressure, as though a hose had just been switched on, full blast. Zed angled it at the attacking mercenaries, dousing them with scalding water. A chorus of screams went up. Blue energy hissed and fizzled out as the guards retreated.

"Adam!" Mr. Adlar skirted the fallen Y. rex and sprinted over to join his son. "I managed to shake off Bateman. Let's get out of here."

Zed reacted to the familiar voice, shuffling backward. "Dad. Got Dad."

Mr. Adlar looked up, unafraid, into the creature's clouded eyes. "Yes, Zed. You got me."

"Ad. Dad." Zed opened his gruesome, gory jaws and reached into the side of his mouth. He hooked out something small and rectangular and dropped it on the ground at Mr. Adlar's feet.

Adam gingerly picked it up. It was the framed photo of him and his dad he'd taken from the flat. The one he thought that Zed, consumed by hate, had devoured. But he'd only been storing it in one of those pouches in the flesh of his cheeks. The glass was cracked and bloody, but the picture was otherwise intact.

The dinosaur's voice was raw and weak. "No Zed."

"No." Mr. Adlar pressed a hand against the dinosaur's battered, bleeding face. "I'm so sorry. Sorry for all that's happened. But thank you . . . for Adam. And for coming back."

"Dad." The word sounded like it had been wrenched from one of the dinosaur's wounds. "Zed . . . Ad—"

The sight of an ominous shadow stopped his words.

"Look out!" Adam saw that the Y. rex had risen again.

Zed turned and roared full force at the Y. rex. But the creature held its ground. It shifted its weight from foot to foot, snapped its teeth and let loose a gut-clenching screech, like some insane, inhuman declaration of war.

"Go," Zed said to Adam, any tenderness in his eyes now lost.

"What about me?" Bateman shrieked. "My legs are busted up! I can't move!"

Mr. Adlar turned to Adam, uncertain.

"Don't leave me!" Bateman yelled again. "Help me, and I'll watch out for you. I'll see you get out of here alive!"

The Y. rex turned to him, as a human might turn at the hum of a mosquito. Adam clutched hold of his dad's arm as Y raised its scaly foot over the fallen man.

Bateman screamed.

The impact—a quick, wet scrape of flesh on rock—was fast and sudden. For Bateman, everything was over.

"Good riddance," said Adam's dad hoarsely.

One victim gone, the Y. rex unfurled its wings and turned its attention back toward Zed.

"Go! NOW!" Zed growled, his own gory wings beating in time with Y's. The steady slicing rhythm built like a menacing soundtrack, louder and faster.

Y. rex rose into the air, followed by Zed. They looked weirdly graceful despite their size and dripping wounds, circling as if gusted on a ghostly breeze.

Snarling and spitting, Y swooped in, reaching for Zed's throat. Zed dodged aside, but smashed into the wall, shaking the Ring with the impact. He tore more cables from the wall, two as thick as pythons and spewing yellow sparks—Y knocked them from his grip and lunged again for Zed's throat, jaws hanging wide.

Zed's going to lose, Adam thought fearfully. Seeing the fight for real and not on a TV screen brought home the scale of the conflict, the sheer, pounding damage of each strike and counterstrike. The creatures' roars were like pealing thunder. A rain of rubble fell from the vaulted ceiling.

"Come on, Ad." Mr. Adlar took his son's hand and started to haul him toward the doorway where the high-pressure steam was beginning to dissipate. "We can't help him."

"And we can't leave him either!" Adam yanked his arm away, staring up in horror. Y. rex had seized Zed's bad wing again, clawing and biting. Zed was weakening. He managed to rip himself free—but the pain and effort left him tumbling into a nosedive. Adam closed his eyes as Zed piled headfirst into the base of the wall. The shock waves knocked Adam off his feet, and he prayed it was stone and not Zed's bones he heard splintering.

When he dared to look again, he saw Zed lying in a crater, crumpled and still. The dinosaur's eyes were closed. Hovering above like some grisly angel of death, Y. rex gave a grim howl of triumph as debris and dust rained down from above. Chunks of rock struck Zed's prone body, but he didn't stir.

Mr. Adlar pulled Adam around, yelled in his face. "This place is falling down around our ears!"

"I don't care! Zed saved us. He—" Adam broke off as the Y. rex swooped down from the shadows to land beside its prey. "Get up, Zed," he said quietly, almost to himself. "Please, don't let it end like this. Get up."

Mouth wide open, Y made ready to bite chunks from Zed's neck. Zed, his eyes barely open, raised both clawed arms and gripped hold of those heavy jaws, trying to force them back. But slowly, inexorably, Y. rex's huge, ivory teeth were edging closer to Zed's throat.

"Please," Adam whispered again. "Please."

"Come *on,* Ad." His dad's grip was harder now; he meant business. He hauled Adam through the haze of steam that hid Zed and the victorious creature from view.

Defeated, Adam ran with his dad along a wide, deserted access tunnel, matching him mechanically, pace for pace.

"The Y. rex will have our scent now," Mr. Adlar

panted. "It won't stop hunting us. We've got to find weapons, more guards."

Adam stared at him blankly. "Now we want to *find* the guards?"

His dad nodded. "They're the only ones with the firepower to hold that thing back."

"Sorry, Bill. The guards have gone." A suited figure stepped out of the shadows a few meters ahead of them.

Hayden.

He seemed confused, swaying from side to side like a man concussed, or in shock—or who had lost it completely. He was holding a gun.

Adam almost laughed—as if a gun could scare them, knowing what was coming up behind.

"Let us pass, Jeff," said Mr. Adlar quietly.

"Perhaps I should. Everyone else has given up and run out." Hayden gave a short, bitter laugh. "Samantha, the technical staff . . . even Bateman! He must've taken his mercenaries with him."

"Your guards may have gone, but Bateman's dead," said Adam. "Your precious Y. rex killed him, and now he's about to finish off Zed while you stand here—"

The sound of a massive explosion came crashing from the far end of the tunnel. The lights flickered alarmingly, and several went out.

Mr. Adlar whirled around as smoke ghosted into sight. "Must be the electrics—all that steam. . . ."

A familiar bloodlusting howl sounded, crawling down the corridor in successive echoes.

"Y. rex," Adam breathed.

"It's not over, you know." Hayden spoke with unnerving calmness as the lights buzzed on and off overhead. "Geneflow has so many projects in preparation, right around the globe, no single setback can stop us. Survival of the fittest, that's the name of the game—and *we* will decide who's fit to survive." He raised the gun to cover Mr. Adlar and smiled. "Now, come on, Bill. We can still turn all this around."

Adam glanced behind, feeling a familiar prickle of gooseflesh as a dark, bestial shadow padded into view.

"For God's sake, Jeff!" Adlar shouted. "Let us pass!"

"Swear you'll work with me willingly," Hayden said, pointing the gun at Adam. "Swear that you'll see the project through till the end."

The dinosaur came forward into the flickering light, its body battered and bloody, its head sooty and scored with scratches. And Adam's heart capsized in his chest at the sight of the beast's bared ivory-dagger teeth, which were all very much in place. Which meant that this was definitely the Y. rex.

And that Zed was dead.

"All right!" Adlar wrung his hands together. "I swear I'll see it through. Now please . . . he'll kill all of us."

The hulking, scaly monster narrowed its eyes and quickened its step. It was horribly close now, a wrathful growl building in its throat through tight-clenched jaws.

"It's all right, Bill." Hayden waved his gun. "I made that thing. It can't touch me." As the Y. rex strode ever closer, Hayden barged angrily past father and son to yell at it. "You hear? There's not a thing you can do to me, because I learn from my mistakes. I adapt!" He nodded. "Your predecessor turned against me, but you can't. Because I had Josephs place one overriding priority command into your brain: You—Can't—Hurt—Jeff—Hayden. Not ever."

The creature's huge jaws swung open. Then it froze dead in its tracks.

"Yeah, you're feeling that conflict in your brain right now, aren't you?" Hayden turned to face his two prisoners and smiled. "I plan for every contingency. See?"

I see something, thought Adam, staring past him at those terrible jaws. His pulse quickened. On the upper right-hand side, five or six of those dagger-pointed teeth were *sliding out* from the swollen gums.

"You want to know why I'm a natural leader?" Hayden went on arrogantly, gesturing at the frozen monster. "*That's* why."

The loose teeth fell to the floor with a bloody clatter as the dinosaur shook its head.

"*Not* Y," it hissed.

Before Hayden could even scream, the monster's mouth was around him, snapping and tearing at his body, crushing bones and swallowing flesh and clothing until there was nothing left.

Mr. Adlar put his hand over his mouth, white-faced. "Project's through, Jeff."

"Zed?" Adam whispered, reeling with emotions he hardly knew how to name. "Is that really you?"

The dinosaur wiped his grisly mouth and sank to his knees. "All . . . done . . . ," he growled, as gore went on pooling from his wounds. Then Adam and his dad had to hurl themselves clear as Zed pitched forward and struck the concrete floor.

With a final flicker, the overhead lights went out.

24 ENDING

Twenty-four hours later, Adam was sitting in a deserted common room, glad he would soon be gone from the shelter. Partly, that was for safety's sake; the place was designed to withstand a nuclear attack, not a clash of killer dinosaurs and massive explosions in the heart of the complex. Several walls and ceilings were already showing the strain, crisscrossed with cracks or spilling plaster and rock dust.

Ironic that Y. rex's attack on Edinburgh Castle had, in the end, given Zed the means to save himself, thought Adam. The bomb that Y had not deployed had gone back into the pouch in its cheek. From his poking around in the gory evidence, Mr. Adlar realized the bomb had gone off and taken Y's head with it. Zed must have primed it while his clone was struggling to bite him, then kicked the creature clear.

The injured reptile had even thought to take Y's shattered teeth and use them to disguise himself as his identical twin. Adam shook his head in grossed-out wonder. *Another fine Zed strategy,* he thought grimly. *Brutal, cunning—and successful.*

You said it yourself, Hayden. Survival of the fittest.

Still not quite sure how he had survived this ordeal himself, Adam longed to escape the whole Frankenstein setup and get back to familiar surroundings again. The weird machines, the hum and buzz of their workings . . . they were freaking him out.

Adam supposed it was lucky for Zed's sake that the shelter was so well equipped. Weakened close to death, the dinosaur had been helped into one of Hayden's bioregenerators to recover. For such a high-tech miracle it didn't look like much—basically a large vat identical to the one Zed had hurled at his attackers back in Fort Ponil.

If we'd only known then where the journey would take us. . . .

His dad said it wasn't safe for anyone else to stay in the room with Zed while treatment was in progress. So Adam tagged along while his dad checked the rest of the shelter for anyone who might be injured.

Or for anyone who might know where Josephs had gone.

"She's not likely to come back here, is she?" Adam asked nervously as they sat in the common room. "And if she ever does . . . well, with Hayden and Bateman both gone, she can't cause much damage."

"Sam Josephs believed in Hayden and his ideals absolutely," his dad said. "She'll most probably be making for one of the Geneflow facilities. Lending her expertise to another of their little projects . . . or helping them to abduct another specialist."

Adam chewed his lip. "They won't come after you again, will they?"

"I'm sure they'll have other priorities right now," Mr. Adlar said carefully. "What worries me more is the bigger picture. These people are organized. Well financed. Ruthless."

"And building more dinosaurs," Adam murmured.

"Experiments in evolution," his dad agreed. "But what are their real aims? What are they working toward?"

"Nothing good." Adam sighed wearily. "Jeez, wouldn't it be good to feel properly safe again?"

"Which reminds me . . ." His dad looked at him. "Josephs told me you were New Mexico's most wanted before you skipped continents."

"Oh, no, I almost forgot!" Adam jumped up from his chair. "The police won't be after me, will they?"

"Well . . ." Mr. Adlar paused dramatically, and then smiled. "Nah. Bateman's phony evidence didn't stand up more than a couple of days. The police called off their manhunt already."

"Dad!" Adam whacked him on the arm. "That isn't funny!"

"Just figured you'd like to know." Mr. Adlar's eyes met his. "We might never be 'properly safe' in this world, whatever's out there. But if we're together, things are better . . . right?"

"I guess so." Adam couldn't find it within himself to smile back so warmly. "But you know . . . things can't be like they were, Dad. I can't just tag along behind, while you go off living your life. 'Cause it's my life too."

"I know." His dad nodded. "I've learned that. From now on, we do what's right for us both." He held up his fist. "Deal?"

"Sounds like the right kind of evolution to me." Adam knocked knuckles with him. "Deal."

o o o

Zed's treatments went on for hours. While his dad sifted through Hayden's files and records in the War Room, Adam dozed fitfully on a couch in the corner. It felt strange, sleeping on something soft after so many long nights roughing it.

"Can we go back to the flat soon?" Adam asked when he finally woke up.

"I want to," Mr. Adlar told him. "I just don't know what I'm going to do about all these research materials, all this equipment. . . ."

Adam pulled a face. "I wish we could blitz the whole lot."

"But if it was used differently, a lot of this stuff could benefit humankind," his dad argued. "Do I have the right to destroy it?"

A brute voice grumbled from the doorway. "Zed does."

"Zed!" Adam turned to find the dinosaur glowering in the doorway. He was looking in much better shape, his scales a lustrous deep sea green, still scuffed and scraped, but with neat, puckered scars where open wounds had gaped the day before. "Are you feeling all right?"

"Go." Zed's dark eyes shone. "Time to go." His voice was just as deep and gruff but it sounded clearer somehow, less slurred. He braced his back against the entrance to the War Room and strained with all his strength. Thick black cracks ran like rising veins in the wall above him.

"Wait!" Mr. Adlar cried. "I know you must be angry, but you can't just—"

The ceiling split open with a sound like giants' bones breaking. "C'mon, he means it." Adam grabbed hold of his dad and dragged him outside. They ducked under Zed's legs and hid in the relative safety of the tunnel outside as a rumbling noise built and the walls began to crumble.

Seconds later, Hayden's mission control was pulverized, buried under tons of rock, more ancient still than even the earliest dinosaurs.

As the echoes of the rockfall slowly died, Zed carried Adam and Mr. Adlar to the blood-soaked ruins of the Ring. He opened his jaws, and Adam saw new shoots of ivory already pushing through to replace his lost teeth. The dinosaur flew up and sheared through the remaining cables, severing the arteries of power that fed the whole shelter.

Emergency systems kicked in, bathing the place in thin, eerie white light.

"The backup power will probably last for a few days," Mr. Adlar muttered. "After that, the shelter will stay dark forever."

Good, thought Adam.

He and his dad followed Zed silently out through the tunnels to the loading bay, where the massive elevator platform waited to take them to the surface.

o   o   o

They came out in the lean-to behind the sham gas station, in the shadow of Arthur's Seat. The night was surprisingly warm, and a crescent moon hung like a jaunty grin in the dark, clear sky.

Mr. Adlar took huge lungfuls of fresh air, beaming madly with each breath. "It's so good to be outside!"

Adam couldn't be sure, but Zed appeared to be nodding in agreement. He, too, breathed deep. Then he gripped the controls that opened the hidden entrance in one claw, and crushed them into scrap.

Mr. Adlar didn't look back, striding onto the dark forecourt. "I've been kept a prisoner for so long." He stared out over the cityscape. "To be free again . . ."

"But just look at that." Adam pointed to the floodlit ruins where the castle had been. It was as if the whole thing had been carelessly scrubbed from the skyline. Helicopters hovered like fireflies around the ruins that teemed still with the emergency services; the winking lights that crowned their vehicles were like tiny blue flashbulbs going off in the dark.

Adam shook his head. "How can something so real vanish so quickly?"

"The castle can be rebuilt," Mr. Adlar murmured. "The importance of old buildings isn't just in the stones. It's in their story."

"What about Geneflow Solutions—*their* story? Planning and plotting in their secret bases all over the world. Hayden said so." Adam turned hopefully to Zed. "Will you help us find them?"

The huge dinosaur shook his head. "Your world. Not Zed's."

"But if there *are* other dinosaurs, or even other

clones of you," Adam said, "you wouldn't have to be alone."

Zed stared down at him, impassive.

"T. rex wasn't a pack animal," Mr. Adlar noted. "He lived alone. And now he's recuperated properly, he won't have the same confusion in his head about me and you."

"Right. That's . . . that's good." Adam nodded. "But where will you go, Zed?"

"Alone," Zed breathed.

"After all that's happened, I guess I can't really blame you." He pushed out a long breath, forced an awkward smile. "You're your own dinosaur now."

The beast snorted softly. "Go, now. Time."

"I know you'll find your way, wherever you're going," said Mr. Adlar with a stiff smile. "But I hope it's a place where you'll be left in peace."

"*Adlar*. . . ." Zed looked at Adam's dad, his expression unreadable. "Go."

Mr. Adlar looked uncertainly at Adam.

"It's okay, Dad," said Adam.

His dad nodded and retired to a discreet distance, leaving Adam and Zed alone.

"Well. . . ." Adam stared up at the figure that had dominated his every waking moment for so long, thinking back over their adventures. He wasn't afraid anymore. Not of Zed.

"We survived," said Adam.

Zed snorted. "Hard."

"That's for sure," Adam agreed. "There were times when we were that close to—"

"*Stay* close." Zed slowly reached out and pressed his hand to Adam's forehead. "Here."

Adam didn't flinch from the weight of the rough scales against his skin. Slowly, he laid his palm against the back of the huge claw. "See you again, Zed."

Zed tilted his head. "Again," he said. The word lingered in the air for a few moments, like one last secret understood.

Turning then, the Z. rex powered away in long, loping strides. Flicking open his wings, he launched himself into the night. Higher and higher he soared, until his dragonlike form was silhouetted against the moon— that same silver moon that had lighted his way all those millions of years in the past, still shining for him now.

Adam looked down at the impression of scales in his palm. He wiped his eyes. Heard his dad come up behind him. "You okay, Ad?"

"I'm good." Adam watched the shadow on the moon grow smaller, shrinking to a speck. "But once Josephs and her Geneflow friends have been sorted out, I'll be a whole lot better."

"The evidence here has been buried, but maybe in New Mexico . . ." Dad shrugged. "We'll find someone who will listen. Someone who can help. But . . . how about a little rest and a good breakfast first?"

Adam considered. "Sounds like a plan." He grinned at his father. "Sounds like a *definite* plan. . . ."

They set off together through the sleeping city, beneath the ancient stars and shadows of the night, as the dawn made ready to rise.

PHOTO © STEVE BARRY

Born in 1971, **STEVE COLE** grew up in rural Bedfordshire in the UK. He loved reading and writing stories as a child, although at school his teachers often despaired of him—one of them banned him from her English lessons, which enhanced his reputation to no end.

While he still enjoys writing almost anything—from novels to articles to songs to puzzles—he has found his real love is creating children's books. He is the author of the popular Wereling trilogy and *Thieves Like Us*, among many other fiction and nonfiction titles. *Z. Rex* is his first book in The Hunting trilogy.

When he's not writing books, Steve likes to spend time with his young children, make music, and eat hamburgers.

To learn more about the author, visit his Web site at **www.stevecolebooks.co.uk**.